Seascraper

Praise for Benjamin Wood

'Benjamin Wood knows how to generate tension, makes lively characters you can see and hear and writes about rural England in a sensitive, considered way that doesn't stray into the nostalgic. A huge talent'
Hilary Mantel

'A novel that feels as if it has been imagined with slow and tender care – and I suspect will be cherished by readers for a long time'
Sunday Times

'What a writer'
Richard Osman

'Benjamin Wood's Booker-longlisted novel about a young shrimp scraper is easily one of the most beautifully written books of the year. The 44-year-old Southport-born author specialises in working-class loners who are fascinated by human creativity but get dragged down by treachery, madness or something from their past . . . A strange, utterly engrossing tale'
The Times, 'Best books of 2025'

'A tale so richly atmospheric you can almost taste the tang of brine and inhale the sea fog . . . What makes Wood's writing such a pleasure is his attentiveness to the prosaic details of everyday life . . . he transforms the quotidian into the poetic, making the exactitude of each task sing on the page'
Guardian

'Benjamin Wood is a beautiful writer . . . both gripping and unputdownable. Like people in Thomas Hardy, his characters surge from the page'
Andrew O'Hagan

'Wood is a seriously talented writer, able to enter the
minds of his characters with eerie precision'
Financial Times

'A well-wrought novel, whose pleasure is in each
careful scene, moment and sentence'
Irish Times

'A treat . . . Wood's daring narrative decisions show he hasn't lost
the old spark, but has just added to it with his new repertoires'
John Self, *The Critic*, 'Fiction books of the year'

'Highly accomplished . . . it's idealistic, gripping and beautifully textured,
moving with great power. It's rare to see such attention to character
and setting, and I think Wood is one of Britain's best young writers'
Philip Womack, *Spectator*

'Benjamin Wood is building a sublime body of work. This
masterful . . . novel is his best yet. It swallows you up'
David Whitehouse

'Enormously compelling'
Daily Mail

'Lyrical, emotionally charged . . . beautifully gripping'
Evening Standard

'Atmospheric . . . slim but eventful . . . Wood is a precise and
pungent writer who conjures the briny, locked-in atmosphere of
his setting so completely that one half-expects the pages to be stiff
with sea salt and a crustaceous whiff of the catch of the day. The
judges for this year's Booker Prize seemed to agree; they put it on
their longlist . . . Another small but mighty coming-of-age story
set on a remote British coastline breached by swaggering, dubious
outsiders . . . A crowd-pleaser, well-hemmed and radiant'
Leah Greenblatt, *The New York Times*

Seascraper

BENJAMIN WOOD

PENGUIN BOOKS

PENGUIN BOOKS

UK | USA | Canada | Ireland | Australia
India | New Zealand | South Africa

Penguin Books is part of the Penguin Random House group of companies
whose addresses can be found at global.penguinrandomhouse.com

Penguin Random House UK,
One Embassy Gardens, 8 Viaduct Gardens, London SW11 7BW

penguin.co.uk

First published by Viking 2025
Published in Penguin Books 2026
003

Copyright © Benjamin Wood, 2025

The moral right of the author has been asserted

Penguin Random House values and supports copyright.
Copyright fuels creativity, encourages diverse voices, promotes freedom
of expression and supports a vibrant culture. Thank you for purchasing
an authorised edition of this book and for respecting intellectual property
laws by not reproducing, scanning or distributing any part of it by any
means without permission. You are supporting authors and enabling
Penguin Random House to continue to publish books for everyone.
No part of this book may be used or reproduced in any manner for the
purpose of training artificial intelligence technologies or systems. In accordance
with Article 4(3) of the DSM Directive 2019/790, Penguin Random House
expressly reserves this work from the text and data mining exception

Set in 11/13pt Dante
Typeset by Falcon Oast Graphic Art Ltd
Printed and bound in Great Britain by Clays Ltd, Elcograf S.p.A

The authorised representative in the EEA is Penguin Random House Ireland,
Morrison Chambers, 32 Nassau Street, Dublin D02 YH68

A CIP catalogue record for this book is available from the British Library

ISBN: 978-1-405-97524-7

Penguin Random House is committed to a sustainable
future for our business, our readers and our planet. This book is
made from Forest Stewardship Council® certified paper.

For Isaac and Oren,
again and forever

> Beyond the shifting cold twilight,
> Further than laughter goes, or tears, further than dreaming,
>
> There'll be no port, no dawn-lit islands! But the drear
> Waste darkening, and, at length, flame ultimate on the deep.
>
> Rupert Brooke

First Low Water

Thomas Flett relies upon the ebb tide for a living, but he knows the end is near. One day soon, there'll hardly be a morsel left for him to scrounge up from the beach that can't be got by quicker means at half the price. Demand for what he catches is already on the wane, and who's to say the sea will keep on yielding shrimp worth eating anyway. There's all sorts in the water now that wasn't there when he was just a lad. Strange chemicals and pesticides and sewage. Barely a few weeks ago, there was a putrid fatty sheen upon the sand from east to west; a month before, he waded in a residue of foam that reeked of curdled milk as he approached the shallows. Fleeting things, but if you're asking him, they augur trouble – it's been hard to sleep of late. His dreams are full of slag heaps made from rotten shrimp, and he's there in amongst them with a shovel, trying to clear a path.

It's five o'clock or thereabouts. He rises with the sky half-dark between the junction of his curtains, weary with the aches of yesterday. The sea-clothes he peeled off when he came home are slung over the chair beside the open window for an airing: his wool jumper, oiled and mangy at the chest from the persistent wiping of his hands; his trousers patched up at the knees; a shirt gone vinegary beneath the armpits. But no matter. Who'll be sniffing him except his mother and the horse?

He wears clean long-johns and a fresh white vest to balance out the stink; his ma has folded them so small and neat inside the drawer that he could slide them into envelopes and post them back to her. It's Thursday, so a hot bath will be taken when he gets back home this afternoon. A nip or two of brandy will be needed afterwards to dull the sting of his exertions. Sleep should follow then, till suppertime at least.

For now, he scrubs his teeth and dashes water on his face. His eyes are puffy, jellified. Three days' letting whiskers grow has made a scratchy beard – he'll shave it later, when he feels awake enough to hold the razor straight. His ingrown nails are doubly sore this morning, and his knees crack when he walks – it always takes him half an hour to get his body moving properly. He's barely twenty years of age, but he goes shuffling down the hallway in his stocking feet with all the spryness of a nursing-home resident. The bulb inside the kitchen light is faltering again – a quick tap of the lampshade fixes it. He fills the kettle, sparks the stove beneath it, rinses out his flask, and spoons in mounds of instant coffee and three sugars.

His ma is snoring in her room along the hall. The noise is like a pig slurping its feed out of a trough, and if it isn't getting louder every morning then his tolerance is fading fast. Each snagging intake of her breath grates on his nerves. He makes a good strong cup of tea for her, the bag squeezed in the water till it has the look of casserole, and carries it into the gloom to leave upon her bedside stand. She doesn't stir when he clicks on the lamp; he has to prod her shoulder. All the baggy flesh there wobbles with the jabbing of his fingertip, which makes him recognise how long it's been since he last touched another woman. An awful shudder passes through him at the thought – his youth is coming to an end, and all the lasses he has ever kissed could sit around a bridge table.

The crust on his ma's eyes cracks open slowly, and she levers herself up to rest against the headboard, not a word of thank you, just a nod to mark the furtherance of their routine. Her curls are flattened on one side. She seems as tired as he feels. Her single denture bathes inside a glass upon the windowsill; it makes him mindful of those extra sugars in his coffee, all the butterscotches from the corner shop he's chewed in secret down the years. He goes to fill his flask over the kitchen sink, knowing she'll be in her dressing gown and moving soon, to fry some rashers for his breakfast.

The horse needs feeding up and harnessing. He gets into his boots on the back doorstep, rolls a ciggie underneath the rusty canopy his grandpa built from corrugated iron – it's hanging by loose screws, and one more heavy rain could bring it down. He's not repaired it yet, as mending stuff like that requires an aptitude he doesn't have. His talent is for something else – his grandpa would decry it as a waste of time if he were still alive to hear him sing a tune, and if his ma knew anything about the pocket watch he gave to Harry Wyeth in trade for his guitar, then she would make a bonfire of it in their own backyard.

The first smoke of the day is always one to savour, but it feels especially good this morning – he's not certain why. A change of weather's coming, he can sense it in the air, the early dampness of it on his face, the low hang of the clouds beneath the waking sky. It looks an average day for shrimping, but he's thought that many times before and come back with his whiskets empty. Standing tall, he can make out the chimney stacks of Longferry a mile away, a line of upstairs windows not yet lit. What do people have to dream about so deep into the day, if not great piles of rotten shrimp? Where do they all go while he's out labouring on the beach?

The draught horse – a well-tempered gelding he's declined to give a name for superstitious reasons – is expecting him. Its big head juts out of the stable door, awaiting his arrival with the buckets. *Stable* is too nice a word: it's no more than a tin-and-breezeblock shack his grandpa made some time ago, just wide enough to house one animal and all its tack, an eyesore that abuts their cottage to the east. Their backyard is a paddock with a mesh wire fence; great dollops of manure abound in it like molehills. It'll be his task to shovel it and spread it on the rose-beds for his ma, but that'll keep. For now, he trowels some forage in one bucket for the horse and fills another up with water. He carries them along the bald track in the grass and puts them down inside the stable, saying, 'Morning, boy,' and stroking the daft creature's neck. While it drinks and guzzles, he goes out to finish off his rollie and prepares the harness, lifting down the heavy collar from its hook in readiness. It's always a surprise how fast the horse is satisfied and empties out the buckets: a fair-sized animal like his needs roughly thirty pints of water every day, which means a lot of circuits from the stable to the outside tap and back throughout the week. He brushes down its coat to clean away what's left of any grit and sand, then rushes through the sequence of the harnessing, so automatic to him now that he can do the job with bleary eyes and weakened fingers. The horse is gentle and it takes the collar gladly. It'll wait there nice and patient for him while he checks the gear's right in the cart and eats his breakfast.

There's a haze of bacon grease inside the kitchen when he steps back in. His ma stands at the stove, barefooted in a dressing gown that seems to shrink each time she washes it – the hem stops just below her knees, and the old cord's not long enough to tie around her waist without it slipping. There's only half an inch of height between them and just under sixteen years. She's moving like a crab between the gas hob and the breadboard on the worktop, where two slabs of a loaf are lying thinly margarined. The wireless is on, but at so low a volume it's impossible to tell what's playing. She hears his boots smacking the floor, and says, 'What's making you so tardy at the moment?'

'Didn't think I was,' he answers, sitting at the table where she's not exactly set a place for him, just shoved a few days' worth of newspapers away to form a clearing.

'I'd say you're half an hour behind where you're supposed to be.'

'I'm going by the charts. Five forty-two, low water. What's it now?' He checks the wall clock. 'Bugger.'

'Told you,' says his ma. 'It's nearing half past.'

'I'd better get this eaten, then.'

She passes him a loaded plate. The rashers are too hot, so he dips bread into the runny yolk of the fried egg. 'All right,' says his ma, 'don't wolf it.'

But he does – he throws it down as quickly as his mouth can work it over. His ma leans back against the sink and lights a ciggie, watching him through slatted eyelids: it's as if she's seen the neighbour's cat stalking a bird and cannot bring herself to intervene. He sits there eating, wearing her attention for as long as he can stand it. There are certain men in town who'd die of gladness if they got a passing glance from Lillian Flett – he'll never understand the fuss. *She might've piled the weight on, but she's still a very handsome woman is your ma*, these fellas like to say when they come over for a drink, a compliment that stings worse every time he hears it. 'I'll be off to town before you're back – I've somebody to see,' she tells him. 'And I reckon if I settle some of what we owe at Pattinson's, he'll let us have a few more things on tick. D'you fancy mince or cutlets?'

'I don't mind. As long as you put something in the meter – I'm not eating it by candlelight again.'

'There's plenty left.'

'All right, then. Cutlets.'

'Good. That's supper taken care of.'

As she reaches round to knock some ash into the sink, she lifts one foot behind her, showing all the grubby flatness of her soles. She has a callus on the joint of her big toe. Her ankles are so swollen up they give her lower legs the shine of sausage casing. He swears he didn't notice things like this when he was just a lad, but now the house is much too small to guarantee their privacy from one another, and his ma still carries on about the place as though he is a guileless boy who won't mind glancing at whatever parts she leaves uncovered – when the sad fact is, his eyes are drawn to them against his will, the same way they would be towards a burning building or two drunkards brawling in a car park. 'Ta for that,' he says. 'I'd better go and get the cart hitched up.' He's not quite finished chewing, but he stands and puts his plate beside the sink for washing.

'Leave it there, I'll do it,' she says.

'Thanks, Ma. See you later.'

'Don't be stopping off at Harry's on your way back home again. It's Thursday.'

'So it is.' There's little chance of him forgetting. It's her night for playing rummy at the church hall with the ladies she's too stubborn to call friends – she'll not be home till past eleven. The house will be his own, at last. He'll go and fetch his instrument from where he's got it hidden in the stable, wrapped up in the ratty saddlecloth he never uses. He can spend some time beside the fire with his guitar, perfecting his arrangements of the tunes he's learned. Then he can wander over to the folk club at the Fisher's Rest and pay his tanner, have a listen to whichever group or singer is performing – maybe he'll sign up to play, if he can summon up the spirit. 'I'll come straight from the badger's. With a good few bob in hand, if things go right,' he tells her.

'Aye, God willing.'

'See you in a bit, then.'

'See you, son.'

He collects his flask and pecks her cheek on the way out. In the back room, he puts on his oilskins. It'll soon be rain-hat weather, but he stuffs it in his pocket and decides on Pop's old cap instead: his lucky charm. He takes the big tarpaulin with him, too, still bundled in a roll with string, as he was taught to keep it, dry and orderly. The horse seems happy staying in its shelter, but it doesn't get to choose – they're more alike than they appear.

By the reins, he leads it up the path to where he's set the cart for hitching. Half a dozen empty whiskets are collected in the back, which he'll be very pleased to fill, and both the nets are folded in a fashion it won't trouble him to disentangle later on. He finds room for the tarp, as well. The horse stands good and still for him as he makes sure the cart's two shafts are snug inside their loops and everything is hitched up tight. He settles in his seat, a few feet off the ground behind the animal, and takes the reins in hand again. 'Walk on, boy.' He clucks his tongue. They roll out of the yard and through the gate.

At this hour, it doesn't take too long to reach the landing at the beach. Fifteen minutes, riding on a curve until the unpaved track behind his cottage joins with the straight line of Marshbank Road, when there's a sudden clamour as the horse's shoes clip on the tarmac, a soft rubber whoosh from the cart's tyres, and all the disparate houses start to bunch together on both sides, with shopfronts on the corner of each block presenting wares that tempt him into yearning for the things he can't afford: good leather boots, a proper shaving brush, a nice wool suit, thick books with gleaming covers, new LPs.

In his grandpa's day, the shankers all rode out in a procession: twelve carts clopping down the promenade, their horses making such a din it could be heard above the ring of church bells. All those fellas have retired or moved away, and some are in the ground at St Columba's graveyard. He's the only shanker left in town who's steadfast to the old ways. There's more profit to be made by using motor rigs and shrimping further down the coast near Broughton. Motor rigs can trawl a pair of ten-foot nets in deeper waters than he'd ever risk a horse in, catching four or five times more than he can manage. There aren't so many sinkpits to be wary of up there. The beach is sheltered by the dunes. The rigs have custom-fitted boilers on their decks so they can cook the shrimp on board and skirt around food safety regulations, too. His ma – great schemer that she is – thinks he should get a bank loan to upgrade his operation: buy a scrapyard lorry chassis and an engine, add the shed and boiler with a bit of help from a mechanic. But he doesn't have that sort of motivation. He's no empire builder. He's accustomed to Pop's methods and he won't relinquish them so easily. Those ugly rigs are prone to rust, and, if you're asking him, they'd be a waste of money – neither boat nor building, more like someone's outside privy put on roller skates and given a big, panting motor. No, he'd sooner give up shanking altogether than succumb to using one of those.

The promenade is always free of traffic early in the morning. Wind is hurrying the sand along the gullies of the road. In summertime, Longferry is a town where people seem to go on purpose. There'll be day-trippers parading arm in arm here, come July, great lines of coaches parked up in the lay-bys spilling hordes of pensioners in sandals, giddy children dripping ice cream from their knuckles. This is when the shanking season's over and the shrimp are left to breed. It's someone else's playground then, and he can take or leave it. But in early March, it's just another dismal place that folk can pass through on their way to somewhere more appealing, and the beach is where they stop to let their dogs run round.

He brings the cart down to the landing ramp and rides on a diagonal. To the north, the long legs of the pier, aglow with lanterns; to the south, the shores of Broughton and a stretch of grassy dunes receding into marsh. If he hadn't traded in his watch, he'd check how long until the water starts to rise again, but it's not hard to reckon it by sight when you're accustomed to the job.

For now, the sea is just a faint grey runnel, two and something miles away. He rides on undulating sand that gives beneath the wheels as readily as butter. Biting wind and mizzle on his face. There's no one else to talk to but his horse, who cannot answer back, and wouldn't say a thing worth hearing if it could. Great whorls of steam rise from its flanks as it goes trudging on, the rattle of the harness making accidental music. He keeps his eyes trained on its shoulders, heedful of the slightest change in its behaviour or its gait. There isn't any sureness to the ground hereafter and no promise that a hoof will not land false somewhere and drop. A draught horse could be seventeen or eighteen hands and it might still find trouble in the channels of Longferry. There are sinkpits all across the beach, if you go far enough to reach them. They can drag your horse down by the fetlocks till it cannot move, and if no one is there with you to pull it free, you'll have to cut the straps and leave it there to drown. It happened to his grandpa half a dozen times in nearly sixty years of shanking. There's no sense in getting soft about a horse when you've been raised on tales like that.

Even in the best of weather, it's infuriating graft. He knows that he'll be out here on his own for a few hours, drudging with the seagulls in his ears and shitting on him from above, repeating the same motions as the countless days before. It bores him worse than it exhausts him. Now and then, he'll let his mind stray, whistling out a tune or coming up with different verses for 'The Jolly Waggoner', but when he's less attentive to the job, mistakes can happen: like a decent catch escaping from his nets because he didn't tie the dadding lines up tight. That's just the sort of thing that costs you time and money, gets you scolded by your ma when you return with nothing for the coffers, and she won't be shy reminding you of how you failed her. If your concentration goes out here, you're at the mercy of the unexpected. Habit's all you can rely on.

Now he's out a mile from where he started, give or take, and he can see it up ahead – the sea's white lip, another mile away. The sight of it is more familiar than the wisps of his own breath upon the air. It never used to foul his mood this much, the cold, the loneliness, the graft, but that was long before he harboured any aspirations for himself besides what he was raised to want. He used to think it was enough to fill the whiskets up with shrimp each morning and accept the cash for them by afternoon. Providing is surviving – that's what Pop would tell him, and what else should any man desire? Perhaps a wife, if he could find one that'd have him. Roof above his head. Big pantry cupboards stocked to keep his loved ones fed. A special drop of brandy now and then, and evenings in the pub. Well, surely he could do no better with his life than that? Except, these past few years, he's come to understand: he settled for too little. Everything he puts his mind to when he isn't on the beach – rehearsing songs on his guitar and rearranging them – that's when he feels most alive, that's when he's at his best. If you were to put him in a league of great cart shankers, he'd be rooted to the bottom. Not a soul will ever look at him and think, *My God, that fella catches shrimp so well, it takes my breath away* – he's very sure of that. But soon he'll muster up the nerve to walk on to that little wooden stage inside the Fisher's Rest, and he's got confidence they'll put their pints aside and listen when he sings. They might just clap and cheer and tell him afterwards: *We never knew you had it in you, lad.*

The horse's backside sways in front of him. He lights a rollie, smokes it down as they trek onwards for another mile, and by the time they reach the water's edge it's nubby in his fingertips. He whoas the horse and tugs the reins. 'Wait on, boy. We'll set our nets and get this over with.' He climbs down to the shining sand, feeling its wet patter underneath his soles. The sea has left it dimpled, but the beach here is untouched; the only footprints are his own. He slides the boomer in the gap behind the horse's hindquarters – it's just a wooden spar that ranges out to hold the nets – and fixes down the latches. He hooks the nets on, spreads them on the shore to set them, making certain that the dadding lines are cinched up tightly at their heads. Before he gets back in the cart, he feeds the horse a wedge of carrot for its troubles, rubs its nose. 'All right, finish up, we've work to do. You'll get another when we're done.'

He settles in the cart again and clucks his tongue until the horse is wading in the sea, knee-deep. As far as he can tell, they've got about two hours before the water rises. He might coax four decent passes from the horse – at best, four stints of trawling in the shallows, roughly thirty minutes at a go. He'll let it rest out of the water while he sorts the catch. There's always lumps of coal and twists of kelp to riddle out and toss aside. A lot of tiny crabs and jellyfish and baby plaice: no good to anyone. Sometimes, there are stingerts that'll spike him through his gloves: he hates those buggers most of all. The nice brown shrimp are all he's looking for. The grown-ups, not the young 'uns – he'll be sifting those away and putting them straight back – but as many of the good 'uns that'll dance into his nets he'll take up to the badger's yard and trade for market price.

The first pass is straightforward, though it doesn't garner much reward – just under half a whisket, and the rest is debris and unwanted fare. On the second pass, the rain begins to thicken, slapping on the horse's back. He pours some coffee in the big lid of his flask and slurps it down. His fingers are already numb with cold inside his gloves, and it's a struggle to release the dadding lines when he brings out the nets. The horse is rarely prone to shivering, but now it's standing with its tail tucked in, which worries him. Pop used to feel around a horse's kidneys if he ever got to doubting it was warm enough – he goes to stroke its back and finds there's such a radiating heat he doesn't want to take his hands away. He gives it one more carrot wedge and rubs its nose to pep it up a bit.

The second catch is dire. He fears it's going to be another of those awful mornings when the haul will be so meagre that his ma will send him out again come evening time. Two low tides a day means two good opportunities for earning, after all. It wouldn't be the first night of his life he's had to do it, working under lanternlight, in fog that's sidled in from nowhere, or in gusts of pea-sized hailstones – he's endured a lot of dismal weather just to satisfy his ma. She keeps a tally book of what she owes to folk in town, which bills remain outstanding every month, and somehow she can spread his money out so thinly that their debts are never settled but the bailiffs don't come knocking. One day, when the shrimp are gone, she'll have to overlook her pride and go on National Assistance. They'll be straddling the line of desperation come the summer.

On the third pass, there's a stronger pall of rain and he's compelled to put his oilskin hat on. Pop's cloth cap is drenched. There's nothing but the dregs of tepid coffee in his flask to drink. He cranes his arm into the back for the tarpaulin and unfurls it to protect the gear inside the cart. The horse is showing him no sign it's spooked enough to give up trawling yet. 'We've seen much worse than this, boy, haven't we?' he calls, repeating one of Pop's refrains as though the horse would know the difference, and they keep on going. Little waves are shouldering the cart's tyres, spitting upwards at his face. The sea is patterned by the rain like honeycomb. He's trying to make the best of it, but he can tell the horse is getting more reluctant. Soon, it gives a nervous snicker and refuses to go on another stride. He tugs the reins and clucks his tongue, but nothing happens. 'Walk on, boy, walk on now.' The horse rebuffs him. 'What's got you so het up?' He climbs down from the cart into the water, standing shin-deep in the swell. Then he wades round to gather in its bridle. 'Shush now, what's the bother, eh? It's just a bit of weather.' He gives its nose another stroke to soothe it, but the horse is panting at him, still resisting. Trodden on a rock, perhaps. It's looking miserable, and he can't say he blames the creature for it neither. 'Let's be having you,' he says, and draws the horse out of the water by the reins. Once it's on the firmer land again, it seems much happier. He inspects its legs and undercarriage. 'Reckon you've just had enough of doing my bidding for the day, you lazy pony.'

He stands there with his hands upon his hips, deciding what to do. Rain attacks his head, descends his peak, and makes a muddle of his thoughts. He wipes his brow and gazes at the sky. It's bleak, as though a lightning storm is coming, which they say a horse can sense. 'All right, fine. We're finished. But you know I'll have to work you twice as hard when we come out again.' The horse appears impartial to the news. It has no better plans. 'Let's bring you in, and we can get packed up.'

He leads it further inland by the bridle, slow and steady. When they're far enough upon the shore, he turns to get the nets – it's so reflexive, how he moves upon this beach. He's been making these same motions since he was thirteen, as weedy as a lad can be, in Pop's enormous oilskin trousers, tied around the waist with rope to keep them up. The pattern is ingrained so deep in him he almost doesn't register the sight before his eyes. *Hang on.*

His nets lay sprawled upon the beach like two collapsed balloons – the first one, on the windward side, is clogged with some dark lump. A hefty clot of shrimp and kelp and little fish are captured with it, too. He ambles over, hunkers down to get a proper view. 'No wonder you were getting in a twist,' he tells the horse. 'You're dragging up scrap iron.' It's a mercy that the nets aren't torn to shreds. But when he lifts the object out, it's not the rubbish he's expecting: it's a rusty metal box, about the size of Ma's good family Bible, with fasteners at both ends like on a Kilner jar. The rain sounds dull and fat upon the lid. There's some strange mass inside that slides each time he tilts it.

Now the horse is getting twitchy, wanting to be dried and fed. 'All right, settle down, I'm coming.' He finds a place to stow the box inside the cart and tucks the tarp around it, then he hurries back to empty out the catch. The leeward net is fuller than he's seen it in a while. His fingers move as fast as he can make them work upon the riddle, throwing out the dross and saving all the plump brown shrimp. Despite the great palaver, it's a decent haul. He's got two whiskets filled up by the end, which is an average day at sea; if he were greedy or more desperate, he would keep the horse out for another pass, but he's quite glad for what he's got and eager to be out the rain. He pats the horse's shoulder. 'That'll save another trip tonight. Good on you, boy.' He gathers up the nets and folds them in the back, pulls in the boomer. The briny water and the rain have made his nose run something awful. As he turns the cart for home, he snorts a jelly disc of phlegm into his throat and spits it at the wind. It tastes like varnish smells.

He hears the clatter of the metal box as they go riding through the milgrims, over all the ridges in the sand and jouncing on the driftwood. It occurs to him that they could shelter for a while beneath the footings of the pier so he can give the horse a rest and something of a feed before they head off to the badger's to get paid. He'd like to have a peek at what's inside that box. His mind is playing a daft projector reel of treasures he might find. Perhaps his luck is changing. How much does a gold bar weigh? How much a bag of diamonds? He permits himself to wonder how he'd spend that kind of fortune, pulling on the left rein so the horse makes its slow arc towards the pier.

It takes a while to reach it, and he's aching for a smoke and a long drink of brandy by the time they're parked below. His skin feels gnawed off by the wind, his lips chafed raw. He studies the damp boards above his head. It's strange how quiet it is without the rain upon him. He wrings the water out of Pop's cloth cap. There's just one rollie left inside his tin: he digs it out and lights it. The horse accepts the last few carrots and he dries it with the shammy cloth as best he can. It's steaming like the boilers up at Rigby's place, all breath and sweat. The rollie does the same for his own constitution – gentle warmth is spreading in his chest with every drag. He climbs into the cart and pulls the tarp away to let it drain on to the sand. The box lies at his feet, a rusty bulk.

Even through his gloves, the edges are so rough and brittle, and the clasps will not unfasten, so he pokes around their hinges with his fillet knife till they release. Inside, he finds a heavy bundle, something wound in manky cloth. The wrapping comes away as simply as a bandage. When he sees what he's uncovering, he stops a moment, sensing trouble like the horse did in the water.

He removes a stubby-looking gun – black metal, scratched across the barrel, with a grip made out of Bakelite. The sea has not corroded it too much: it can't have drifted round for very long out there. Either it's been dumped or lost by accident. It hinges open in the middle, and he finds it's loaded with a shell as broad as a cigar, brass-capped. He studies it awhile, as though he'd know one pistol from the next. It looks to be a flare gun. There's a decent chance it fires, but he's not keen to try it out right here beneath the pier in daylight. It'd only scare the horse. The simplest course of action is to throw it straight back in the sea, but he's still holding on to it, for reasons he can't understand, enjoying the heft of it against his palm. Perhaps it's worth a bob or two. Would Hinkley take it at the pawnshop? Doubt it. How about that bloke who works the cellar at the Fisher's Rest – McMahon? He'd know about this sort of thing. McMahon is always shifting bits of stolen gear out in the car park from his van. For now, he wraps it up and shoves it in the box. He hides it underneath the nets and tucks the tarp in.

It's a winding journey to the badger's yard on Threlfall Lane. The rain's not letting up. He brings the horse along the foreshore where the shell-scraps lie in wavy piles and crunch below the tyres, then steers it up the slope. They're clopping down the coastal road in no time and annoying traffic – cars are slowing down behind to honk their horns and swear at them from rolled-down windows as they overtake. Some have more reserves of patience, trundling at low speed behind them with their wipers on. After half a mile or so, he turns off at the junction, slipping down the narrow lane between the marram grass and dunes, and following the snaking trail beyond the settlements of bungalows until they're at the tarmacked yard of Rigby's Seafood Merchants.

Seven years he's ridden to this place to sell whatever he can scrape out of the sea – he must've seen John Rigby's face more times than his own dumb reflection in the mirror, except he feels as though he knows as little of him as he does of the New Testament. In his grandpa's day, they'd bring the shrimp back home and boil them on the stove – it was a family business. As a little lass, his ma would sit with all the women at the kitchen table, and they'd shill the blighters as they came out steaming from the pot, until their fingers scabbed up from the peeling – afterwards they'd take them to be potted and sold off at market. But all kinds of fussy regulations have been passed since then, and now it's easier to bring them fresh out of the water to the likes of Rigby, get himself a few crisp notes in hand and start again tomorrow.

One of Rigby's shillers is there skulking in the doorway of the outhouse, smoking underneath the overhang. There's a chequered headscarf tied below her chin, a massive yellow stain along the front of her white apron. Seeing the horse, she throws her ciggie down and scampers off inside to fetch the boss. The trees beside the yard provide no cover from the rain, so he just leaves the cart where it's convenient, somewhere it'll take no effort to turn round. Before he's even got the whiskets out, John Rigby's come to greet him at the threshold with a mug of tea. He's pouring something in it from a hip flask, which is just about the most enticing prospect any shanker could envision in this weather. 'I'll be having one of those, John, while you're at it,' he calls, striding through the yard.

'The pot's still warm. You're welcome to a biscuit, too.'

'I meant the booze.'

'Can't help you there. Medicinal supply. Hands off.' John steps aside and reaches for the door's loose handle. 'Get your bleedin' shrimps in here and hurry up so I can shut this quick. You wouldn't get me out in that for love nor money.'

'Well, your money's fine by me, John. Save the love for someone else.'

The old man sizes up what's in the whiskets with a brisk sweep of his eyes. 'How much've you got there? A quart?'

'I'd say so.'

'All right. Give it here so I can weigh it out for you.'

He passes what he's brought to John, who goes to pour the shrimp into a metal basin on the scales. It's something of a pantomime, because he always pays two pounds, four shillings for a quart, and anything a little over is dependent on his going rate of charity. 'They're not so lively,' John calls over. 'How long since you caught them?'

'Same as always. I just scrape them up and bring them here.' Nobody needs to know about his little wait beneath the pier this morning with the flare gun.

'I dunno – a few of these are sort of – well, they're squashed and mangy-looking.'

'John, they're shrimp. You needn't put them on the telly. Boil them up and pot them.'

'Customers are getting picky over that, you know. We've had complaints.'

'From who?'

'The people we supply to.'

'You can have the mangy ones for free, then. Pay me for the rest.'

'All right. Call it, what, two pound?'

'You're lucky I'm too cold to stand here bickering.'

They shake on it. John brings the grubby notes out of his apron pocket, holds them up. 'Suppose I'll see you here again tomorrow, lad.'

He takes the fella's money with a sigh. 'I can't see why you wouldn't.' It's become their everyday farewell. He's getting tired of it. His empty whiskets are still on the table by the scales. He fetches them and heads out to the cart. 'Take care, John. Ta-ra.'

'Aye. See you, Tom.'

The journey home is blustery and slow. He watches swathes of drizzle going left and right as he comes up the coastal road. The horse does not complain, although it's sprayed by all the passing cars. It seems to take an age to reach the promenade again and get away from traffic. Once they're in amongst the buildings of the town, the wind is off their backs, and he considers stopping on the corner for tobacco, but thinks better of it. He's aware of his own graduating stink. The foulness of his armpits has been made worse by another shift at sea. He wants to get indoors beside the fire, fill up the bath and soak in water nearly scalding hot. The horse could use a drink and all.

Eventually, the ground gets softer underfoot. They're back upon the track that leads to home, slow-wheeling by the houses of his neighbours, all the folk his mother used to know so well when she was little, who'd not raise their heads to look at him if he should ride across their paths today. Some people are so righteous in their minds they can't accept mistakes in others. They would rather cradle condemnation at their breasts than help someone in trouble. He can't understand that kind of bitterness at all. There go the Cannings, in their cottage with the chimney flooding smoke – no word from them in twenty years. There go the Spooners with the overrun front garden, and the Gordons with their grandkid's pram left in the porch – nary a hello since he was born, not even after Pop died. They're just phantoms he's been told exist. A silver car is parked up on the verge outside the Gordons' gate. He ogles its interior, all the walnut and green leather, wondering at the cost. Their eldest girl has married well, according to his ma. It must be true if they've a fancy Humber to be gallivanting round in.

His front gate is wide open, so he rolls the cart straight through and up the side path, then he trudges back to close the latch. The horse stands, fidgeting a bit, while he unhitches all the gear. It shakes its lips as he takes up the bridle and escorts it to the stable, strips off all its tack and lifts away the collar. Once he's dried it off some more and got it currycombed, he fills up its two buckets: water first, then half a scoop of forage in the other. It's an indoors-loving horse, this one – whoever heard of such a thing? Well, it can rest for now, but when the rain dies off, he'll bring it out to graze around the paddock. He's got several jobs to do before he puts his feet up: all the dollops of manure to spade away, the gear to organise inside the cart, the wheels to hose down and wipe off.

When all of this is done, he goes in through the back way, kicks his boots off on the step to let his ingrown toenails breathe again, and hangs his oilskins up. It's only as he pushes at the door into the kitchen that he sees the lights are on inside – the faulty bulb is pulsing, so he walks right up and hits the shade until it stops its flickering. He thought his ma would not be home when he got back, but he can hear the thump of chatter in the house, as though she's left the wireless playing. He can't make out her words. He calls, 'Oi, Ma – you home?' The dishes have been done. A stranger's overcoat is draped across the chair. She's left a butcher's parcel on the counter, bound with twine, as thick as *War and Peace*. How many cutlets did she manage to finagle out of Pattinson? Enough to feed them for a week. He's putting water in the kettle at the sink when he first hears the laughter: someone's low guffaw. It comes again: *ha-huh, ha-huh*. His ma has got a visitor.

He feels a heavy dread inside his belly, traipsing down the hall to the front room. There's nothing he wants less than to be civil to some fella with designs on getting in his mother's bed, but that's what must be done. His mood is dark, and he's not apt to hide it, but he'll have to introduce himself. 'I'm home, Ma,' he calls out, 'where are you?' But he knows exactly. She'll be perching on their sofa in her finest clothes, a tray laid out upon the little table: all the cups and saucers that she saves for best, the milk jug, sugar bowl, a dish of biscuits. Her guest will be beside her with his legs hinged outwards, one knee glancing hers, an arm upon the cushions at her back. He'll have a paunch about him, jowls, bad teeth, an eager face turned gloomy by the sudden interruption. Every fella like the last one. He could paint a portrait of her type, and she deserves much better than she thinks she's worth. But this is not the picture that he finds when he comes through the door.

She's all alone upon the sofa in a cardigan and frock, no lipstick on, her hair not even brushed. And he can tell from the alertness of her eyes that she's enamoured with her company. The fella's kneeling by the fireplace, jabbing at the edges of the coal-bed with the poker, talking at her with his face towards the hearth: 'It's dumb, I know. We used to argue over who would get to light the fire at home – my father always got his way, of course, so now I take great pleasure in the job.' Is he a Yank, this fella? Talks like one, all curly-ended, nasal. Standing tall, he looks about six four. The smoke is thickening behind his legs. He takes a hankie from his trouser pocket to wipe off the soot. 'Oh, hey,' he says, and flicks his eyes towards the door at last. 'I guess you must be Tom. It's good to meet you.'

Now his ma says in a kindly tone that's just as foreign to his ears, 'Come in, love. Don't just hover in the doorway.'

It's a pointless dance, and he's not keen to hear the music or to partner up. 'Look,' he says, 'I need a bath. I'm knackered. Reckon you could do your courting somewhere else?'

The fella seems a little stung, as though he isn't used to being spoken to in earnest.

'Thomas Flett,' his ma says, 'don't be rude.'

'Excuse me, but I need a bit of privacy.' He gives the Yank a freighted look.

'I think you've got the wrong idea,' the fella says. 'If there's a problem, I can come back later. Really, I don't mean to inconvenience you.'

'Don't be daft,' his ma protests. 'It's not his living room, it's mine.'

'I pay the bills,' he answers back.

'That doesn't make it yours.'

The fella stands there, blinking at him meekly. He's wearing modest clothes: a knitted jumper with a cotton shirt and rumpled trousers, scuffed black brogues. 'Your mom said I could wait for you. I'm sorry if I'm getting in your way, but I just had to come and introduce myself. I'm not in town for long. They want me back in London in a couple days – you folks don't have a phone line, so I thought I'd just stop by and see if we could start a conversation.' To his ma, he adds: 'We'll have to get a line put in. He's going to need a phone.'

Who *is* this fella? He's never heard someone so smitten with the sound of his own voice. There's something disconcerting in his self-assurance. But he's quite a striking man to look at, in an awkward sort of way, with deep-set eyes as brown as bladderwrack, his dark hair combed in floppy waves, two wispy sideburns with a tinge of grey. The knuckle of his nose has once been broken but it's given him a sage and weathered sort of charm. There's no doubt he's a notch up from the usual fella who comes calling.

'Did you see those steaks out there?' his ma chimes in. 'He brought them as a gift for us – they're rib-eyes – so you'd best sit down and let him talk. As long as you've been breathing, you've not eaten meat that good. The least that you can do is listen to the man.'

He supposes he should muster some politeness, but he can't surrender or he'll never get his house back. 'Ma, I stink. I need a bath.'

'D'you really think I'm bothered what you smell like? I've been sniffing you since you were born. Get over here and sit.' She pats the empty space beside her on the sofa, widening her eyes at him until he does as he is told. It doesn't matter if he lives to be a hundred, she will always hold the reins and he will always get the bridle. When he's next to her, she wafts the air and says, 'You *are* ripe. Blimey.'

He ignores her. 'What's all this about, Ma?'

'If I may,' the fella says, and lowers himself into the rocking chair, which nobody has sat in since Pop passed away. It's too late to refuse – the rockers are already creaking underneath his mammoth frame. 'My name is Edgar Acheson. You might've heard of me before, I won't presume you have. It's best if I just say I'm in the movie business – but the *business* part is none of my concern. I've never cared how many people go to see my pictures, only that they're good, and you can throw a washcloth over all the guys in Hollywood who think like me. But here I am, still making films. I'm like that funny fish who breathes on land, the – what's it called? The mudskipper. That's me. Somehow, it stays alive despite the odds.' And there it is again, that self-admonishing guffaw. He rocks back with his fingers steepled for a moment, till his face regains its sombreness. 'I've come to offer you a job, Tom, if you'll hear me out. I saw you on the beach when I was driving up here yesterday – *could not believe my eyes*. I thought I was hallucinating. Well, I've had to hunt around to get your address, but I'm not a man who gives up easy. And I figured I'd come see if you were home this morning, but of course you weren't. Your mom was very kind to let me in, though – she's good company, your mom, I like the way she thinks. We drank some tea and talked a little bit about the things I'm looking for. And she's confirmed it – you're the man I want. So what d'you say, Tom? Can we talk about it, you and me? I figure we could pay you something in the region of a hundred pounds, but my producers can discuss those numbers with you further down the line, if you accept the gig. It's two weeks' work, beginning June sometime. Well, three weeks', *tops*.' He laughs again, but quietly, more an exhalation. 'Sorry, I should let you get a word in edgewise. This is how I get when I'm excited for a picture. Swear to God, I've only had two cups of tea. I guess your mother makes it pretty strong, huh?'

'Strong enough to chew,' his ma says. 'How the Lord intended.' Once she's shucked the pleasure from this joke again, this joke she's made a thousand times before, she notices the quiet in the room – it seems to shame her. 'Thomas, did you bite your tongue or what? He's offered you a hundred quid and you've not said a word.'

'I heard,' he answers, 'but I don't believe him. No one's paying me that sort of money for no reason.' Down the years, he's sharpened his awareness of what's bluster and what's truth; it's usually the men who talk like factory chimneys, huffing out their words in spumes, that have no substance to their claims – and these are normally the types who fool his ma to parting with the final shilling in her purse before they disappear. This fella has that way about him.

'Smart,' the fella says, 'I wouldn't be too quick to trust me either. You're my kind of guy, Tom. Let me check if I can find something to – hang on just a sec.' He reaches deep into his trouser pockets to retrieve his wallet – 'Okay, this should do it' – and extracts a slip of paper that's been folded up in there so long its seams are limp and faded. 'I don't give too many interviews – I hate reporters – but I spoke to somebody at *Life* a few years back. I carry it around because my daughter's in the picture with me and I like the shot of us. I really miss her when I'm on the road. Is there a date on it? Let's see. Okay. No date. It's obviously a few years old, because Louisa's more grown up now, but I guess it's something. Here, Tom, catch –'

The folded page is thrown up in the air but only falls between his feet. He picks it up and gets it open. It's a printed photograph, ripped loosely from a magazine. There isn't any doubt whose face is pouting back at him, a fist propped underneath his jaw, a camera dangling from his neck. The only difference is the haircut, which is cropped much closer on the sides. His freckly daughter has an arm around him, sitting on his knee. The caption underneath appears legitimate. *Above: Director, Edgar Acheson, for whom* THE CUTTING PARTY *marks an overdue return. Below: a rare day off, at home with daughter, Louisa (12).* He shows it to his ma, who brightens at the sight of it and says, 'How old's your daughter now?'

'Sixteen,' the fella says, 'I think.'

'She's very pretty.'

'Thank you. I agree, but I can't take the credit. She's my wife in miniature.'

He doesn't care much for the way the fella's eyes rove left and right when he is talking – it's as if he's trying to catch a fly that no one else can see. 'All right, Mr Acheson,' he says, before things get too cosy, 'I don't trust you've got a hundred quid for me, but I'm prepared to listen.' He refolds the page and holds it out; the fella has to get up from the chair to grab it. 'Not *illegal*, is it, what you're asking?'

'It's as kosher as it gets.' The fella grins. 'But first – please call me Edgar.'

'No, thanks. Mr Acheson is fine for now.'

'Well, suit yourself, but you pronounce it *Atch-eson*. Not *Aitch-eson*, like you've been saying.'

'Good, because my name's not Tom like *you've* been saying – it's Thomas.'

Mr Acheson is flushing slightly, though it seems he's more astonished than embarrassed. 'Now we're getting somewhere. I can see we're going to get along just fine.' The chair's still rocking and he doesn't sit back down. He stoops over the mantelshelf and runs his finger on the spines of all their paperbacks, the best of them reclaimed from jumble sales and church bazaars for pennies. 'I can't stand to be in houses with no books in them, can you?'

'I've never really thought about it.'

'Thomas doesn't go to people's homes,' his ma chimes in. 'He's either working or he's reading. Sometimes he might go the pub with Harry Wyeth. Not often. I can't get him out the house, and we don't even have a telly.'

'That's a thing we've got in common, then. We're solitary types,' says Mr Acheson, and turns to peer right at him – into him, more like. 'You ever read *The Outermost*? It came out in – oh boy, I guess it must be twenty years ago already. Well, it had a different title to begin with, and it didn't get so much attention. So they put another cover on the next edition, called it something else – *The Outermost* – then people seemed to notice it existed. Funny how that goes.'

He's not familiar with the book. There's half a chance he's seen a copy of it on display in Hughes's window down the high street, passing by. 'Can't say I've ever heard of it.'

'Don't worry. Not a lot of people have.' Mr Acheson tilts out some worn books from the row, considers them approvingly, then puts them back. 'I read the thing in manuscript and – I don't say this often – it completely stole my heart. I thought it wouldn't sell, and I was proved correct on that, but I still got the feeling it'd make a marvellous film. No problem getting hold of the rights, believe me . . . Well, the screenplay took some time to get tuned up, and now I'm finally going to make the picture. We're in pre-production at the moment. Wheels are turning.'

He's been getting used to sitting on his hands till Mr Acheson has finished talking. 'What's this got to do with me?'

'It's like I told your mom –'

'He's going to film it on the beach – in Longferry,' his ma breaks in, as giddy as a girl in clover. She's brushing off the armrest with her palm – it's only when they've got a visitor that she seems conscious of the mess.

'Not all of it – just part. But probably the most important scenes,' says Mr Acheson. 'It has a lot of sequences that happen on the beach in fog. I mean, it would be simpler just to shoot it on a sound stage down at Elstree with some fog machines, but that'd look too flat, too fake. We scouted a few beaches out in France and Yugoslavia, but I wasn't so convinced by them. It needs a certain kind of atmosphere, this picture, so I had to put the feelers out a little wider. There's a DOP I know who used to come here as a kid – he tipped me off about this place – and he was right. It's perfect *and* it's cheap. When I was driving up, I had the strongest feeling, like a *déjà vu*. And then I saw you out there, miles away. I had to get my zoom lens to make sure, but there you were, just riding in the water in your cart – and, holy shit, I almost fainted.'

'Tell him why,' his ma says. She gets up to clear the dishes, stacking them into a pile. 'I'm going to put those steaks on for us. Wait until you hear this, Thomas . . .' And she stands beside him with the tray in hand, apparently electrified by what she knows, the private thrill of it.

'You really have to read *The Outermost*,' says Mr Acheson.

'I'll get a copy to you right away. You'll understand it then. And I've got storyboards at home that would completely chill your bones if you could see them. Do you have a bookstore here?'

'We do. There's Hughes's,' his ma says. 'It's very dear. Just tell him what the film's about, go on. The way you said to me.'

'All right. If you think it helps my case.'

It cannot be the first time Mr Acheson has summarised the story of this book, but he explains it with the zeal of someone who's discovered it at breakfast. 'Well, the novel has a lot of characters and viewpoints, but I'm focusing on one – the village undertaker. He doesn't have a name in the original, but I've called him Runyan for the sake of clarity. I'm hoping Henry Fonda's going to play him, but I guess we'll see about his schedule. Magnus Fielder's said he'd do it – and we've worked on something else before – but he's my second choice for this.'

He talks in frank, decisive bursts, which seems to be his way for everything, and interrupts himself with points of detail, speaking of *diffusion* and *low-contrast filters* and a thing called *magic hour*.

'The picture's set around the eighteen eighties, somewhere on the coast of Maine, but we can't shoot it there, because they'd tax us to the hilt. The whole thing's focused on this foggy little town where everything's a bit unusual, and Runyan's not your normal undertaker either. After someone dies – the baker's wife – he's paid to take her body, and he rides her out to sea. No kidding. Runyan has a horse and wagon just like yours. Well, sort of like it. Older. Anyway, he lays her in the back of it and rides her out for miles and miles. About as far as he can go. About as far as you were out there when I saw you yesterday. The water never gets above the wheels. Eventually, he meets a shore. He's landed on a sandbank. There's a settlement, a little row of huts lit up by fires inside. He leaves her body on the shore. And when he turns around, he sees a bunch of primitives have come to get the body, and he waves at them but they don't give him a response. Next morning, he goes back to pick her up – she's waiting on the beach, bone dry, in all the clothes that she was buried in. He takes her home without a word, and she just carries on with her life, as if nothing has happened – pretty soon, we start to see how things have changed, though. She's got all these new abilities for things: like drawing, singing, making dresses, painting. No one finds it strange except for her. It's how it's always been in this weird village. It's another kind of world. The dead can be revived and they've got knowledge that they didn't have before. Like speaking ancient languages or playing chess, that sort of thing. It carries on this way till Runyan kills himself – he leaves instructions for his burial, but no one understands quite where to go and they get lost in all the fog and die. Now everyone who dies in this strange village dies for good, and nothing is the same. They need to find a way to bring back Runyan and . . .'

The longer he goes on describing it, the more complete the film appears, as if it's just a matter of assembling the right people in one place to realise his vision. When he's finished, Mr Acheson sits down again and rocks himself beside the fire, a stolid look upon his face. 'So, Thomas, what d'you think? Will you be part of this? I need a guy who knows the beach, the tides. Insurance reasons, mostly, but I also want someone who understands the way of life out there.'

'He'll take the job,' his ma says, 'even if I have to drag him by the ankles.'

'There's no need for that. I'll do it.' He can't help but grin, though he's not sure at what. There's now a cool, soft, effervescent feeling in his blood, a sense of possibility that's spreading from his heart down to his ingrown nails. He's always been suspicious of excitement – nothing he anticipates is ever worth the wait or turns out quite the same as he expects – but still, it's coursing through him like a medicine. If it's true that better luck will come to you through patience and determination, he's not felt the benefits of that approach so far. But Pop would often tell him how you had to stay alive to opportunities in life, to never fail to notice when they tap you on the shoulder – and it seems he's being tapped. 'I ought to warn you, though,' he says, 'it won't be easy filming on that beach. It's not a place for cameras and what have you. And it's not exactly somewhere you'll be keen to stand around all day. It's miserable and windy and it's freezing half the time. There's sinkpits everywhere if you go far enough – they're not for taking lightly. Get your timings right, mind you, there'll be a decent fog out there most nights, and I can help you cope with all the rest.'

Mr Acheson folds up his arms. 'It's meant to be. I really feel that. Honestly, I can't wait to get started.'

His ma says nothing more. She turns and gives a little hum and carries out the tray. Her feet go pattering along the hallway.

'First things first – I need some photographs to work from. What's the soonest you could take me out?' says Mr Acheson at once.

'Well, next low tide, but –'

'When is that?'

'Just after six this evening. But it's dark by then. We're best to wait until the morning. First low water.'

'I'm not sure. It might be good to see it in the darkness. Let's do both.'

'I can't. I've other plans tonight.'

'Like what?'

There comes a clatter from the kitchen so familiar to his ears – the base of his ma's frying pan upon the stove. She's such a heavy-handed cook. It won't be long before she's got the wireless going, and the scorched-lard smell will clot the house and overcome his foulness. It's a wonder anyone can stand to share the room with him. Pervasive sweat and shrimp-rot, fish guts, crab flesh, seaweed, dander, forage, gull shit, horse dung – so much filth is clogged up in his pores and gummed beneath his nails. 'I've something else to do, that's all.'

'Okay. What if I could pay you fifty now, up front?' says Mr Acheson.

This gives him pause. The folk club at the Fisher's Rest begins at eight, and if he wants to play tonight he's got to put his name down on the list by quarter to. Perhaps it wouldn't be so bad to wait a week, rehearse his songs a few more times before subjecting people's ears to them. He's not in a position to refuse that kind of money. 'I dunno,' he says.

'All right, fine – I'll give you the full hundred.'

'Blimey. I can't brush you off, can I?'

Mr Acheson guffaws again. 'I told you – this is how I get. It's been a long time in my head, this picture, and I never thought it could be made the way I wanted. Now I've worked it out, and I'm not going to waste a moment I don't have to.'

'If I had more gumption, I'd hold out for twice that much,' he says, and gets up to his feet. He ferrets in the dresser drawers until he finds a packet of his ma's Pall Malls. 'You're lucky I'm so reasonable. I'll do it for a hundred, I suppose.' This constitutes more money than he's made so far this year from shanking, but he doesn't let the thrill of it disturb his voice. He slides away the fire screen, reaches down to light his ciggie.

'That's just great. Will you accept a cheque?'

'You'd better ask my ma. It's her name on the savings book, not mine.' They shake on it, and Mr Acheson's enormous palm encases his; the thumbnail has a bruise, like it's been hammered. 'Are you staying in town somewhere?'

'I'm at the Metropole. It's not so bad. Nice view.'

'Ma used to work there for a bit.'

'Oh yeah?'

'She couldn't stick it out, though.' He can hear orchestral music drifting down the hall. 'If you walk along the road from there a bit, I'll pick you up at five to six. You'll see a kind of statue on the coastal road – can't miss it. Wear a proper coat, and gloves, too, if you've got them. I can bring you oilskins so you don't get sodden.'

Mr Acheson nods back at him. There's something in his stance that reads like apprehension, but perhaps it's more the jitters of enthusiasm. 'Thank you, Thomas. I'll be there. Will you have room for some equipment? Nothing heavy, just a few small cases.'

'I'll make space for what you need. I'm on your shilling now.' He isn't getting any pleasure from his ma's weak ciggies. But he's got some rib-eye steaks to feed on and a tub to soak his bones in. A big payday's coming, too. Life's not so bad for once. 'If you'll let me have my front room back, I'd like to get this stink off me. Was that your car out in the lane? The Humber?'

'Yeah, that's me.'

'I wouldn't leave it there again. It's half across the neighbours' gate.'

'I guess I didn't know where I should park it.'

'That's all right. It's just those neighbours aren't so friendly to my ma, and I don't want to give them anything to gripe at her about.' Fatigue has settled deep into his limbs. It's nothing that hot water and a brandy can't work loose. He clears his throat. 'You're standing where I put the tub. We've only got a tin one and it takes a while to fill it.'

∽

He was thirteen when he first went out to sea with Pop and, in those days, few adaptations to the old equipment had been made – the cart still had two wagon wheels with metal rims, and he felt queasy after half an hour of riding in the seat with him. It was supposed to be a weekend job, that's all, and it was something he would beg his ma to let him do, believing it to be a rite of passage. Every other Flett had been a shrimper, going back to his great-grandpa who had putted barefoot on the beach alone with just a push-net and a basket on his back. But soon enough, depending on the patterns of the tide, he found that he was shanking in the cart with Pop before the school bell every Friday. Then it spread to every morning but for Sunday. Then it spread to Sundays, too.

He didn't feel it was too much to bear, because he had no other interests in his life except for reading, then – his grandpa used to let him do that in the cart sometimes, when it was drier out and they were on their break. He must've swallowed half the library in that time, his favourites being *White Fang*, *Burning Daylight* and *The Count of Monte Cristo*, in whose distant settings he could sense the tangled fabric of himself, some yearning to be faraway. In school, they had begun to study Coleridge's poem about the ancient mariner, and he was drawn to its inherent sense of doom, its melancholy, more than any other text they were obliged to read. There was a pamphlet of it, carbon typed and doled out by the teacher at the start of term, and he looked through it every night in bed. He found that certain lines would surface in his mind like prayers when he was out at sea, and he would murmur them by accident sometimes for his own entertainment – *The silly buckets on the deck, / That had so long remained, / I dreamt that they were filled with dew; / And when I awoke it rained. / My lips were wet, my throat was cold, / My garments all were dank; / Sure I had drunken in my dreams / And still my body drank* – till Pop would clap him hard between the shoulder blades and say, 'Stop mumbling to yourself. You're giving me the willies.'

He was fifteen when his grandpa had his first collapse. His ma had found the old man prostrate on the bathroom floor. She'd shouted, 'Thomas, run and fetch the doctor!' and he'd phoned up from the neighbours' house while they were standing dazed in their pyjamas. It was just a minor stroke, the doctors said, once Pop was in the hospital – they reckoned he'd recover over time with bed rest and a change to his routines. Well, he was back to shanking two weeks later, but he got frustrated with his limitations. 'I can cope,' Pop said, 'but I'm much slower than I used to be. We'll catch more if it's you and me together, so your schooling's got to stop. Not saying it's for good, but I can't earn as much like this – my arm's so gammy I can hardly bring the nets in. Water's at my waist before I've done two passes. If I fill a whisket, it's a blessed day.' So that was it for school. His ma took on a maid's job at the Metropole Hotel along the seafront, and they gave her extra hours at the wash house down in Broughton.

It seemed that they were always scraping round for bits of money, even on the days the shrimp were plentiful and wodges of the badger's cash would fatten up Pop's coat on their way home. But it was hard to glean the thoughts that occupied his grandpa's mind in ordinary moments out at sea. They never found much else to talk about besides the job at hand. Communication in the cart was either terse instructions barked out in the wind or it was fruitless grievances about their paltry catches, quarrels over why the rightful way of doing things could not be questioned – such as, why did Pop refuse to wear his gloves when he was sorting through the catch so that his fingers often bled, and why not wear an oilskin hat when it was raining to keep water out his earholes? Just because he was accustomed to his habits was no valid explanation. All these gentle bouts of bickering would end with Pop reproving him: 'I think it's time you learned the difference between wondering and whingeing, lad,' his grandpa used to say, or: 'Why d'you always have to think so bloody much?' And if they ever stumbled into proper conversation, Pop would shrivel into silence, sniff some mucus back into his throat and launch it at the beach. 'You're like your bloody mother, you are – yapping all the time. We're not out here to chinwag. This is *graft*. Get on with it.'

On certain days, he'd have to chisel scraps of guidance from his grandpa on the things he didn't understand – the right technique for riddling, how to tell which shrimp were big enough for keeping, in what fashion he should braid the ochred twine to mend a net – and he assumed this grudging attitude of Pop's was meant to coax him into solving these great mysteries on his own. He had no instinct for the work at first, and shambled through his tasks with fingers half asleep. But there were idle moments in the cart when Pop's advice would come unprompted now and then; or else he'd get so irked by daft mistakes that he'd be forced to give a lecture, sputtering the words so fast and hot they couldn't go unheeded.

When the fillet knife went missing from the bucket underneath the seat, for instance. Pop had made him turn his pockets out to prove it wasn't him; but it was him all right, and he'd withstood the screaming rage that followed. 'Let me tell you why that knife stays where it is – why smart-arsed boys like you can't go round moving things that aren't for moving. Are you hearing me, 'cause sometimes I do wonder . . . Turn and have a look there, where I'm pointing. Set your eyes on the horizon, where that flock of gulls is flapping round. You see it? Straight line to those dunes across the bay. I'd say it's just about a hundred yards from there, north-east. Well, that's a big old patch you never want to let your horse go near. A proper sinkpit – that's just *one* of them. I write them down, the big ones, when I see them. Keep a chart of them at home. The sand's got arms in different places, see – if you're not careful or you're stupid, you'll get dragged below. The horse'll go down first, and then your cart. It's quick, that sand, like nothing you'll have come across before. So if it takes you, well, you're going to need a sharp knife in a hurry, let me tell you. Cut the straps loose off the horse and pull it free, or let it pull *you* free. But if you reach down underneath the seat into the bucket and that knife's not where it ought to be – that's it, you're done for. Those few seconds that you've wasted have just killed your horse and maybe you and all. So let me ask you this again, son. Where's that knife supposed to be?'

The charge that he was smart-arsed was repeated often in their house. His grandpa would accuse him of being more concerned with stories in his books than with the weight of shrimp inside their nets; one morning, he discovered half the pages from his *Moonfleet* had been used to light a fire, as though in retribution for a bad day at the beach. For years, he shouldered the great lump of an idea that Pop resented his intelligence or found his interest in the wider world somehow condemning – but it wasn't that at all. Whenever he brought home a book, his grandpa fumed in silence at the sight of it upon the shelf, because it served as a reminder of the person they weren't meant to talk about – his father, Patrick Weir.

All he really knew of Patrick Weir was that he'd been a History teacher in Ma's school. It would've been of benefit to him to understand his father's nature in more depth – if he was quick to temper or laid-back like him, if he was weedy or athletic or just somewhere in between – but, as a lad, he learned that it was better not to raise the topic with her, as it always seemed to make her pink-eyed and upset with him throughout the week. Instead, he needled Pop for information, and, occasionally, a drop of truth could be extracted from the fits of his exasperation. 'I don't like to have him in my mind at all, if I can help it. But I'll tell you this – you're right. He's dead and buried. Years ago. I wish I'd done the job myself, but then he joined the army and the Germans beat me to it. Good for them. I hope it was a rusty bayonet and all. The fella didn't even know that you were born.' That's how his grandpa had explained it to him, yielding to his questions one day in the cart when there was nothing else to talk about. He was learning how to bear the torpor of his life at sea then, not just trying to master the techniques. His mind was full of notions of returning to his schooling, doing something different with his life than scraping up the shallows. He was hoping he might find a better calling in his blood. 'Don't ask me what your mother saw in him. He was supposed to be her teacher and he got her in the family way at fifteen years of age – I reckon that's as much as anybody needs to know about the man he was. You're not much older now than she was then – imagine it. A nasty piece of work. That's all I've got to say about him. Don't be asking me again.' He never did, although he made the trip to Broughton town hall once to see if he could find the name of Patrick Weir amongst the war dead. There it was: two faded words inside a dusty ledger.

It was Pop who raised him up when lesser fellas would've left him in an alley or abandoned him at sea. Pop kept on through the shame of it, withstood the damage to his friendships and his reputation in the town, and never flinched when all the draughts of gossip swirled below their door. 'Don't you listen to 'em, Thomas,' he would say, when lads at school began to goad him, 'they're not worth the upset. Kick 'em in the bollocks. They'll not bother you again,' and that'd soothe him quicker than his ma's embrace or any of her sympathetic words. There might've been a lot of disagreements with each other down the years, discomfort at the subject of his birth, his softer temperament, his ways of thinking, but he's never doubted who to thank for keeping him alive and teaching him the methods to endure. He only understands the dangers of the beach because Pop trained him what to look for. All the channels where the wet sand tends to belly on the surface, trembling slightly in the daylight or the beam of his night lantern. Subtle incurvations no one else would give a second look. Without this knowledge, he'd have nothing to distinguish him from any of those mindless fellas in their motor rigs, and Edgar Acheson would not be sitting at his kitchen table, listening to him reminisce out loud.

'The first real sinkpit that I saw was frightening. We were riding to the shallows from the landing, same as always. Then Pop starts to whistle at me. *Stop, stop, stop.* He's spotted something near the milgrims – that's the word he used for all the deeper ripples in the sand, don't ask me why – so we jump down, a distance back, then walk on maybe ten or twenty paces further. Pop says I should crouch down with him, so I do. And I'm not really sure what I'm supposed to look for till he's pointing at the ground and saying to me, *D'you see it? Just a littl'un, that. But think of it ten times as big and you can understand the bother it'll cause.* I mean, the sand looked wet, that's all. No different from the sand around it, but he goes, *Hold on now, keep your eyes down, watch. It's wobbling. See that little wobble?* It looked spongy, like a kidney pudding. *Right*, he goes, *stand back and you can see what happens when I throw this in* – and then he hurls a stone. It falls straight through and splashes up a massive slop of sand. *A shallow one*, he says. *You might get trapped in it, but only to your waist. That's not the point though, is it? Now you know I wasn't joking. Always got to have your eyes peeled when you're out here. I've known shrimpers walk out on this beach and not come back.*'

In other situations, he would polish up these stories to reflect Pop in a saintly light, but he's not shy about the truth today: his grandpa wasn't perfect and that's all right to admit. He's never had such appetite for conversation. There's an open-handedness to Mr Acheson which seems to tease out every knotted thought inside his head. 'I hope that didn't happen to your grandpa – sinking sand,' their guest says now, wiping his long fingers on the tea towel Ma has laid out on the table as a napkin. 'It sure wouldn't be the way I'd want to go.'

'You needn't worry – I can keep you out of bother, easy. I've still got that chart he made, and I've been adding to it now and then. It's all in *here*.' He jabs his forehead with his finger. 'No one knows that beach as well as I do. I can spot a sinkpit from a mile off.'

He can feel the afterglow of bathing, still. His neck is ruddy from the scrubbing brush and razor-burnt. The greasy goodness of the steak is in his belly and he's mopped up all its bloody juices with a slab of bread – he can't remember feeling so invigorated by a meal in years, not merely satisfied, but strengthened.

'Well, it weren't the sand that did for him,' his ma says bluntly. 'It was the infection in his bladder. Not sure which is worse.'

This prompts an awkward silence, and his mind returns to all the empty pews inside the church and no one at the grave's edge but the vicar and two gormless fellas leaning on their spades; and he recalls the lethargy that seemed to flood his body afterwards, the static of the house, the nasty odours from Pop's sea-clothes mouldering in the basket. He would rather not remember.

There's a trim of fat on his ma's plate which she's been saving. 'Are you eating that?' he says.

'Go on, you have it. I feel stuffed.'

He picks it up and champs on it, not bothered by the noises he is making in the presence of their guest, who folds his arms and looks away. Their windows are opaque with condensation, but the daylight's straining through the ribboned streams upon the glass. Mr Acheson leans back and pats his stomach. 'Really kind of you to let me stay, but I should probably get going. A lot of things to organise before we head out to the beach tonight. Some calls to make. I'm grateful to you, Lillian, for the feed.'

'They cooked up pretty well, I thought.'

'Sure did. I'm ten pounds heavier than when I came in.'

'Thanks for going to the trouble. Makes a change from cutlets.'

'Not at all. They were a bribe.'

'Aye, well. They worked.' His ma takes to her feet and starts collecting plates. She gives their guest the gladdened look that usually sets upon her face when listening to her Sunday quiz shows. 'Thomas,' she says, leaning on the word, 'why don't you fetch that chart and show him? It'll help to put his mind at ease.'

'Oh no, I've overstayed my welcome here already,' Mr Acheson protests, but meekly. 'I should hit the road.'

'He'll fetch it – it's no bother, is it, Thomas?'

'No, Ma.' But the truth is, he's not looked once at that chart of Pop's for months and he's not sure if it's still in the cardboard envelope below his bed or somewhere in the mess of papers in his room that Harry's scribbled on: a hundred different chords for him to learn, peculiar names of racing dogs he ought to back, the words to early ballads he might think about performing (like that puzzling one about a farmer who believes his wife is cursed). He tells their guest: 'I'll go and dig it out for you.' It's lucky that his traipsing steps don't draw his ma's suspicions, but she's too preoccupied with Mr Acheson, whose shirt cuff has a stain she wants to dab with soapy water. 'Give it here, come on,' she's saying, 'or it'll ruin.' By the time he's found the envelope – it's buried in a layer of dust below his bed – she's handing Mr Acheson his coat. The table's not yet cleared, but there's a space for him to spread the chart and smooth its folds. 'The darker circles are all Pop's. That doesn't mean the sinkpits are still there, mind you, but that's where they've been spotted. All the other marks are mine. Not seen one for a good few months.'

Their guest peers down and gives a prayerful sort of nod. 'This must've taken quite a bit of work. Looks like the biggest ones are further west, huh?'

'That's the way it is.'

'I guess it's riskier than I expected. But a little danger doesn't put me off. The best locations always have their challenges to overcome. That's what I need you for.'

'As long as you're prepared for what you'll find out there,' he says, 'I'll see you right.'

The chart is just a handmade thing his grandpa copied from the Ordnance Survey map in Broughton library, modified for purpose. All the contours of it used to make him think of spiderwebs when he was younger; now they seem to him more like the swirling lines of his own fingertips. He used to study it most afternoons, in awe of Pop's great draughtsmanship; today, it doesn't seem so accurately drawn, perhaps it even comes across as crude. 'I'm sorry if I made it sound a bit more – I dunno. More *scientific* than it is. It served my grandpa well, at least.'

'I'll bet it did . . .' Their guest has lost his cheer all of a sudden; he's now peering at the chart with the intensity his ma applies to scrutinising apples in the grocer's basket. 'D'you know what it reminds me of? The recon maps they used to give us in the war. The most important thing was knowing where the danger was, and where your enemies were hiding. Give me substance over style, that's what our CO used to say, and that's advice I took to heart, believe me.'

'Were you stationed over here?' his ma says, all the keenness warbling in her voice. 'I never had you pegged as a GI. An airman, maybe.'

Mr Acheson keeps quiet for a moment, then he's moved to answer. 'Sure, I served here for a little while. They had me out in France and Belgium, mostly. Then Korea.' He fastens up his coat with short, stiff movements. 'You could say I did my bit. I'm sure you did yours, too.' He fixes every button to the top rung, and it's only when he's no more left that he admires the chart again and jabs a finger on its edge. 'So what's this here – the triangle?'

'Oh, that'd be the fogbell house,' his ma says. 'Down near Broughton.' She explains that, in the old days, men would walk out on the beach for miles barefoot, pushing nets by hand through all the milgrims, where the shrimp were happiest. 'We called them putters. Lots of them'd wind up stranded when the fog got thick. The coastguard had to build a fogbell house to stop it happening. Paid a bloke to sit in it at ebb tide every day. A proper little brick hut with a stove inside, you know. A comfy chair, some booze. I reckon I'd have liked that job myself, but anyway. This bloke'd clang the bell up on the roof to guide the putters back to safety. When they started using horse and cart instead, it wasn't needed any more. The bell's not even in it now. Some bugger pinched it for the scrap.'

He'd assumed that Mr Acheson was only listening out of courtesy, but he was wrong. 'That sounds like something I should take a look at.' His stiff finger's prodding at the chart still. 'If it's derelict, then all the better. No red tape to cut through, and it might be good for what I have in mind. A nice aesthetic detail. Could you take me out there later?'

'I could take you right away,' his ma says. 'If you drive us there. It isn't far.'

'You sure about that, Lillian?'

'Well, you might be better off with Thomas.'

He can already foresee the outcome, should he let his ma drive off to Broughton with their guest. Her way of getting more acquainted with a fella is to bleat at him about the wondrous things she could've been if she'd not had a son to raise and if the pains of labour hadn't wrecked her body so. There'll come the well-intentioned tales about her baby's endless thirst for milk and how he wouldn't leave the breast till he was old enough to set the table, all the small embarrassments that mortify him, which she seems to think are proof of her resolve: his fussy eating patterns and his infant rashes, and the pages of her women's catalogues gone missing down the years. He's not prepared to watch it happening again. 'I'll take you, Mr Acheson,' he says. 'Just let me get my boots on and I'll come out to the car.'

'Terrific.'

'Well, all right, that's settled that,' his ma says. 'Gives me time to wash my whites, though drying them'll be a job. I'll show you out the front way, Edgar.'

He can hear them saying their farewells along the hallway while he's fetching his good coat and tying up his boots. The mizzle clings to him as he steps out. The sky is like a quarry's face, already much too dim for afternoon. He sees the horse's nose protruding from the stable's hatch; its black eyes always seem so peaceful, thankful to be living, and it gives him calm. A motor sparks and idles near the gate. 'Don't have him out too long, love – he's a busy man,' his ma reminds him from the doorway. It's a rare occasion she accedes to using their front entrance, which she likes to keep for best. The last time would've been the day they wheeled his grandpa to the ambulance.

Now the silver bonnet of the Humber creeps along the verge and stops outside their cottage. Mr Acheson is almost wedged behind the steering wheel, his wipers flashing; he scrolls down the window and calls out to his ma: 'I'll have him home within the hour, I promise!' She says something back but it gets lost below the chunter of the engine. 'Jump in, Thomas. Let me put the heaters on. Which way should I be going?'

'Left,' he says, and drops into the waiting seat. 'Smells nice in here – the leather.'

'Guess I'm used to it by now.'

The car rolls off the verge and U-turns, heading up the track to Marshbank Road. He's not accustomed to the easy speed of the machine, the gentler gravity of driving, how the neighbours' privets smudge into a woody paste as they go by. His backside's slipping on the gloss of the upholstery and he has to grab the handle on the door. 'I've never ridden in a motor like it. Harry's got a van, but it's got worse suspension than our cart, and by the time you're out of it, you're seasick.'

Mr Acheson is steering with one hand, his pupils flitting to the gearstick every time he changes up or down. 'You can't go everywhere by horse, you know. The earth's too big.' It's said in an amused way, and it's clear his trite advice is meant to raise a smile. 'But never let a guy say what you can or cannot do. I reshot half a movie once because I didn't like the actor's tie. See, he was playing a public defender, and this thing was always in the shot, this hundred-dollar tie the folks in Wardrobe put him in. I should've noticed it in testing – that was my mistake. They said it didn't matter, but it mattered plenty, so we did his scenes again. It cost the studio a little more, no doubt, but no one had a word to say about that tie in the reviews. They only praised the actor for a great performance. Do I go right here, or straight?'

'Straight on. Then second on your right.' They're on the fringe of town now and the rain's still on the windscreen, soft as sugar. He's not certain what to say about the actor and his tie, although it's plain that Mr Acheson is proud to reminisce about the episode.

'It's quite a dreary day for photographs. I'll probably need a higher ASA than I've got with me. One thing you learn fast in my job, Tom – excuse me, *Thomas* – is to never be without a camera. So I keep an Automagic in the glove compartment, cheap thing, point and press. My good one's always in the trunk, but, stupidly, I'm low on film, so I'll just have to go with what I've got. I guess you have your own equivalents – the knife, like you were saying. The knife's your camera.'

'Nah,' he answers, watching folk grow bigger on the pavement and then disappear from view; a fella twists to get a look at who's cavorting in a car so dear as they glide past. He's used to being noticed, lurching down these roads all week behind a horse in iron shoes, except he's not felt this conspicuous before. 'I could catch a million shrimp without a knife. But I can't be without a horse. I lost a month last year when it got strangles. Nothing I could do but wait for it to heal.'

'That must've put you in the red.'

'Too right it did. I borrowed some and worked it off, month after.' It'd been a kindness from John Rigby that'd seen them through, and he'd gone shanking twice a day until he'd paid him back. 'That's why the horse gets all the rest it needs, and I just have to kip when I can manage it.'

'Perhaps your mother should've taken me instead.'

'I volunteered,' he says. 'And this is hardly work. It's riding round in luxury.' In such close quarters, he's aware of quirks in Mr Acheson's appearance that weren't obvious at home: the restless nature of his eyes, which never seem to settle on an object for too long, and deep-set scars upon the arches of his nose from pimples in his youth.

'Do me a quick favour? Reach into the glove compartment there and see if I've got any rolls I haven't shot yet. Could've sworn I had a couple somewhere.'

He flips down the lid and finds the Automagic camera, not much different from the ones he's seen for sale behind the glass at Hinkley's. There's a paper box marked AGFA that's got nothing in it, and three metal canisters. 'Will these do you?'

'Used, I think. Let's see.'

He passes them to Mr Acheson, who takes the full set in his palm and puts them on his lap. He twists the cap off one and tips out what's inside, reviews it as he's driving. 'Nope,' he says, and throws it on the back seat, picking up another, which appears to rattle as he lifts it. 'Not that one,' he says, and pockets it. 'But good to know I had it.' The last one doesn't satisfy him either and he hands it back. 'Too bad. I'll check what's in the case when we're parked up. Oh hey, my hotel's on this road, I think.'

'We'll pass it on the way. D'you need to stop?'

'Not at the moment.' Mr Acheson's not looking where he's driving now – he's gazing past the limits of the sea-bank, at the grey expanse of sand and solid, shrouding rain. 'I can't believe the sea's out there. I love the bleakness of this place. I've never seen a beach so uninviting.'

'Well, it scrubs up better in the summer. For a day or two, at least.'

'Don't get me wrong, it's bleakness that I'm looking for. It's nothing but a positive.'

'Perhaps for you,' he says. 'The rest of us have got to live here.'

'Yeah, I guess.'

'Look, that's the place I meant before – the statue.'

They rush beyond it much too fast for Mr Acheson to register the sight. 'Oh, was it?'

'There's the Metropole and all.' It's set back from the road, part-screened by pine trees and a timber fence. 'You like to travel round in style. I've never even stopped in a hotel. My grandpa got the use of someone's caravan for us once, down in Wales, but then he wasn't well enough to go. I've heard they do a good roast of a Sunday where you're staying.'

'I doubt I'll eat for weeks after today. My pants are tighter than they were this morning, that's for certain.' Mr Acheson begins to fidget with the blowers, attempting to demist the glass. He puts the radio on, in search of something, but finds nothing to maintain his interest – not the tail end of the jangling song with its brash whooping chorus, not the plummy voices on the news discussing what they all agree will be a scandal for the minister in question. 'Politics – so dull,' he says. 'This world's so full of noise and most of it is pointless.' He twists the dial to switch it off. 'A bit of peace and quiet's what we need here, Thomas. Right?'

The closer that they get to Broughton, the more the sand dunes bunch together on the collar of the road. He'd wander out here as a lad, carefree, and tumble down the slopes for hours with kids from other towns he'd never see again. Back then, he wouldn't give much thought to smashed-up bottles that were dumped there, or the damage he could do an ankle treading in a burrow. He's forgotten that simplicity, that joy. It's true what Mr Acheson is saying about the world and all its noise, but most folk seem to carry on undaunted, just like children gaily sliding down a sand dune. When did he stop sliding for the fear of broken glass and bloody knees?

'It really doesn't seem there's much to do around here,' says Mr Acheson, 'not for a guy your age. Don't you have some place where you can take a girl – a dance hall maybe? An espresso bar?'

'We've got an old arcade with slot machines and things. Amusements for the tourists. But they're shut until the summer starts.' He doesn't know a bar that serves much else than beer and spirits.

'Do you have a sweetheart? Or at least some girl you've got your eye on?'

'Aye, but she's got better stuff ahead of her than me. She's older and – to make things worse – my best mate's sister.' Even thinking of her now, imagining the pleasure of a basic conversation on the subject of her weekend plans, the price of stamps, or Harry's recent haircut, floods his heart with so much yearning he feels pressured, timid.

'Ah,' says Mr Acheson. 'That's quite a bind. But maybe you don't have to be Houdini. You could ask your buddy for permission.'

'I dunno. For starters, it'd help if she could tell I liked her. I just get too –'

'Tongue-tied?'

'No. *Polite*.' He shakes his head in deference to his own stupidity. 'Polite like she's the vicar at Ma's church or something daft.'

'She's not, is she? The vicar?'

'Nah, but lasses don't much like politeness in a fella, do they? Not that I can tell. They seem to like the rogues.'

'I'd say that all depends on who the girl is, Thomas. I don't think I got my wife by being mean to her. Perhaps I tried to be aloof at the beginning, but she only married me because she found me interesting. That's just the type of girl she was – attracted to my lousy personality. It took a few more years to notice my astounding handsomeness, of course.' That deep guffaw of Mr Acheson's is oddly spiriting to have beside him.

As the dunes begin to lower again, the turning shows itself ahead – a rutted track that curves and forms a plane of sand and dirt. It's not a car park if you ask the council, but the constant flow of tyres has fashioned it to serve as one. He points it out to Mr Acheson, who brings them to an empty space and cranks the handbrake, shuts the engine off.

They're faced by sandy knolls, but, on the other side, the sea lurks closer to the foreshore than it rests at Longferry. 'D'you see that pole? That's where they had the fogbell.'

Mr Acheson leans in to squint at where he's gesturing. 'Can we get a little nearer?'

'If we walk a bit.'

'I wish this rain would stop.'

'Don't waste your wishes. You'd do better praying for a good umbrella.'

'In the trunk. I'll get my Leica, too.'

They leave the car and stand out in the drizzle for as long as it takes Mr Acheson to gather his equipment. The umbrella he unfolds is dainty, meant for someone half his size – 'I think this is my wife's,' he says, 'but it'll do the job' – and he ducks underneath the fancy camera's strap and roots inside its case for extra film. 'I've got sixteen shots left on this roll, that's it. I'll have to be more frugal with my eye than normal. Let's get moving, shall we? Lead the way.'

The cold is bracing, which is no surprise, but there's a stillness that's unusual for Broughton. Quite often, as you're walking up to meet the dunes, the grass shakes all around you and the sand moves at your feet in eddies. Not today. It feels as if the softness of the rain has pillowed everything. Not far from here, the motor rigs park overnight, a fleet of them like gypsy caravans, locked up with chains.

Mr Acheson is striding next to him, and keeps on pivoting to take in their surroundings. Step by step, the fogbell's pole grows taller and the rest of the squat building ranges into view. Its bricks are green with moss. The chipboard on its doorway bellies, daubed in marker pen by schoolkids, lovers' names carved into hearts and scratched out afterwards. The roof is sturdy, though, and all the iron rungs to climb the pole are still intact. 'I told you it was just a shell,' he says. 'Not much to look at.'

His companion has the camera to one eye, the stalk of the umbrella pinned beneath his arm. 'It's just a shame we can't go take a peek inside.'

'You'd need a crowbar.'

'How about a tyre iron?'

He isn't certain how to answer.

'I'm just kidding, Thomas. You can take that panic off your face now.' Mr Acheson adjusts the leather strap around his neck. 'I'll settle for a few exterior shots.'

It's something to behold, the skill with which he operates the strange mechanics of the camera, crouching to get what he needs into the frame. The shutter clicks at least a dozen times, then Mr Acheson gets on his feet again, nodding at the building, sighing, tutting, walking round it. 'Well, Thomas, I'm not sure,' he says eventually. 'I just can't say for sure.' His hand goes to the pocket of his coat. 'I'll show my best design guy – he can tell me his opinion from a pure production aspect. Maybe it's a detail we don't need.' He's got the metal canister of film out, screwing off the cap. 'D'you think it's possible to climb up there or what?' His arm extends; he means the pole. 'You ever try it, Thomas?'

'It's a long way up,' he answers. 'Wouldn't really interest me to see the view. There used to be a seat up there, beside the bell. The bloke'd sit there while he rang it. Some life, that. Just waiting in a hut for other blokes to get in bother. I suppose he got some reading done, though, eh?' The fixings for the fogbell have remained in place – the same old brackets from a hundred years ago, still clinging to the timber. When he turns his eyes away, he finds that Mr Acheson is heading to the car. He quickens his own strides to catch him.

'I can't say you didn't warn me,' his companion mutters, chewing on some remnant of the steak he must've just dislodged. 'But I hoped for something – I'm not sure – a little stranger. Runyan's got a workshop where he builds the coffins, and I thought this might just suit. I'm not convinced.' He's running his tongue back and forth across his teeth. 'I'll drop you home. Let's see if we get better luck this evening at the beach.'

'All right.'

He's worried that he's fallen short of expectations. It was daft to take his guest out in this cheerless rain. He should've let his ma go, after all. Her stories would've been a good distraction from the disappointment: how she used to bunk off school to come out here and smoke the dog-ends she'd pick out the gutters, how she'd kissed a lad or two from Broughton Grammar in her day. They walk back to the Humber in near silence.

Once they're in the car and motoring again, the blowers seem to reawaken Mr Acheson's enthusiasm. 'Maybe I can tune this into something worth a listen.' He fidgets with the radio until it's playing a song that he can tolerate. 'You like this sort of thing? My daughter does. Or used to. Hard to say these days what she enjoys.'

It's one of Elvis Presley's ballads. He can't tell one record from another really, just the fast stuff from the slow, the brazen from the sappy. 'I was never all that keen on rock 'n' roll, though I suppose I ought to be. I like traditional music – folk songs.'

'Pretty maidens in the barley fields, that kind of thing?'

He smiles, unsurely. 'Sometimes. More like – there's this group, the Catheralls, who play round here. They're quite well known. Sing harmonies as well as anyone I've heard. Good range of songs and all. And there's another band called Front Foot Forward who do mostly jigs and reels – a fella with a squeezebox and another on the fiddle. They can really get you going if you've had a drink or two.'

'Well, I don't think my radio can pick them up.'

'You'd have to hear them at a proper club. They're worth a ticket.'

'Yeah, I'll stick to Perry Como, if it's all the same to you.' It seems they're driving even faster on the homeward leg. The signs along the coastal road are skidding by. Below the steering column, Mr Acheson's left foot is jittering upon the clutch, as though he's playing a church's organ. 'My father liked that sort of stuff. The real old-fashioned music. Pipes and fiddles. Never did see eye to eye with him. Except about the war – on that, we both agreed.'

He wants to say he never even knew his father, but it doesn't seem correct to drop such freight into their conversation, and what could his companion say in any case? Sympathy's not what he's after, neither's pity. It's a bridge he wants – between Longferry and the world beyond – and Mr Acheson could be the one to help him build it. 'I play a bit myself, you know. Guitar.'

'Oh yeah?'

'I'm getting better at it – slowly, mind. Sometimes I think my fingers are too thick to work the strings. I'm still a bit too clumsy. But it's nice to sing away my worries now and then. It's soothing.'

Mr Acheson's left knee is going like a piston. 'I guess I ought to try that. I can't sing a note.'

'Just don't tell Ma.'

'About your singing? Why?'

'She'd take it the wrong way, that's all.'

'Well, I won't rat you out, don't worry. I can keep a secret.'

'It's not a secret. I just haven't told her yet.'

The peaceful introduction to another song begins, the radio crackling as they meet a patch of bad reception on the promenade. It gives the journey home the feel of Christmas; the familiar sights made different, glazed by all the syrup of the tune. He doesn't think it's Perry Como, but it must be close enough as Mr Acheson's placated by it. They haven't any words for one another till they've pulled up on the track outside the cottage gate. 'Well, I appreciate your company. I'm sorry it turned out to be a goose chase. See you later, Thomas – five to six still good for you?'

'As long as you're still keen to go.'

'You bet I am. I'll be there at the statue, like you said.'

'Ta-ra, then.'

'Try to get some rest, huh?'

'Fingers crossed.'

As soon as he steps out the Humber, he's reminded who he is again. His first thought's for the welfare of his horse, his second is for sleep. He watches Mr Acheson reverse and turn. The engine's thrum is heavy, blotting out the birdsong in the trees. As the car goes down the lane, a long arm ranges from its open window, waving. Then it's just a streak of silver in the distance, lost beneath the cries of seagulls. He can feel his heartbeat in his ears.

The house is darker now their guest has gone. The kitchen's shabby, dim in every corner: has it always been this way? It doesn't have the wondrous sense it had before – the friction of the unexpected. How can he be missing someone he has known for just a few short hours? It can't be said that Mr Acheson is much more than a stranger to him, but already he's begun to hope it might become a friendship. You could knock on every door in Longferry and never find a man as interesting. He doesn't know another soul who earns a living from his talents. There's the painter lady who does funny portraits on the seafront in the summer, but she cuts old women's hair at nursing homes in the winter. Even the best singers at the Fisher's Rest have got a trade by day, and the athletic lad from school who everybody said was destined to be England's centre forward is still playing as an amateur for Broughton AFC and works a lathe in the components factory. But Mr Acheson has seen the world on nothing but the strength of his abilities and vision, and it's rousing to believe that such a thing is feasible. How much imagination does a fella need to build a livelihood upon? A sight more than he's got, no doubt. He can't yet write a song that doesn't borrow from a hundred other tunes. He's never seen *The Cutting Party* or a film with Henry Fonda in it. Come to think of it, he hasn't even gone to Broughton pictures since he took his ma to *Lady and the Tramp*, and she was coughing through it so much that he barely heard a word of what those dogs were saying.

In their warm front room, she's getting on with chores, spreading their wet bed sheets on the drying rack before the fire. She potters round unthinkingly, the way a clockwork mouse will skitter till it needs rewinding, humming to herself. He's never been so vexed by this before. Their life is just a mindless trudge of work with cosy patterns of behaviour in between – he's always known this, overlooked it for the sake of their togetherness, survival. But he cannot stand to watch her keeping up the normal circulation of their days. He wants to wake up every morning with a better purpose.

'Ma, leave that to me. Go on and put your feet up.'

She doesn't seem to hear above the noise of her own humming.

'Ma –'

'It's done now.' She turns round to study him, already guessing his response to what she asks. 'How'd you two get on, then?'

'I don't think he'll use the fogbell in his film. But he was glad to have a look. We're going at low water, still.'

She shrugs, but with her face. 'Well, I suppose you can't have everything.' Their ironing board is up and there's a stack of wrinkled clothes upon the sofa. He can smell the metal tang of the electric iron. 'Listen, don't be saying a word to folk about our situation – no one'll believe it.'

'Who'm I going to tell?'

'There's Harry Wyeth, for one, and he's a loudmouth. Soon as people sniff the money in our pockets, they'll be knocking to remind us what we owe them. And besides . . .' She pauses while she moves the rack a fraction closer to the fireguard. 'I'll be keeping Edgar to myself. I know he's married and I haven't got a chance of anything between us, but he's not your average sort of fella, is he? And he's in our lives, not theirs. He's like a miracle.'

'You'll get no arguments from me on that score.' He gets the iron and makes a start on what's amid the pile: it's mostly his own sweat-stained shirts and bobbly trousers. 'I suppose you won't go bragging to the girls at rummy, then?'

'I wouldn't even share my handkerchief with that crowd. I'll be betting matchsticks with them, same as always, listening to them moan about their husbands.' Now her eyelids tighten with a twinge of pain. 'My back's got stiff again. I ought to go and lie down flat.'

'All right, Ma. I'll see to all of this.' She's been complaining of this problem for as long as he's had ears to listen. There must be something causing her discomfort, but it irks him how it seems to plague her at the least convenient times – when he's dog-tired and bound for bed, or busy mending nets outside, or when he's reached the brightest section of a book he's reading in his room at night. She says she doesn't blame him, but her back's not been the same since she gave birth, which generates a special sort of guilt in him.

'Aren't you going to have a kip?' she says. 'You'll need to brighten up a bit before you go back out again.'

'The horse wants putting in the yard first, anyway.'

'I'll manage with the ironing. Go and sort the horse out now, then have an hour in bed. You can't let Edgar down.'

'You've never cared how tired I was before,' he says. 'I've been in worse condition and you've sent me out to sea.'

'Well, now you've got a boss who isn't me. And he's not paying you a pittance, neither.'

'Don't you worry. I'll not scare him off.'

'You'd better not. I won't forgive you.'

He goes outside and brings the horse into the paddock for a graze. The creature's left a fresh load of manure upon the straw-bed of the stable, so he mucks it out and rinses off his hands. He smokes another Pall Mall, watching the quick motion of the clouds across the melancholy sky. More rain is forecast later, but he doesn't see the makings of it yet. His ma has left the front room by the time he gets back in. She's shut the wireless off and he can hear the gentle ticking of their kitchen wall clock like a dripping tap.

The air inside his bedroom is so thick and stale. He strips down to his long-johns, tries to take his socks off but the wool snags on his ingrown nails; the bath has drawn the pus out of his wounds and it's congealed to form a glue. He peels the mushy flesh away to get the fibres out and lets the pain subside. One day soon, he'll get them looked at by a doctor, but he's coped with them for long enough the urgency has gone.

He gets beneath his sheets and finds the comfy dip his weight has fashioned in the mattress. Sleep is coming – he can sense it, blurry in the outer limits of his mind like weather stirring up the dune grass far away, and he surrenders to the feeling, but it doesn't take him. Thoughts will not dissolve. The conversations of his day repeat and skew inside his head, and he can't stop revising them and wishing he had spoken less forthrightly, been more positive, more likeable, or more refined. He isn't sure how long he lies there, rolling over, rolling back, but the best part of the afternoon is wasting. He accepts that he's too tired to sleep, and gives up trying. Pop always needed brandy to sedate him, and now he's reached the age where he can understand a man's dependence on the drink. There's half a bottle left inside the kitchen cupboard that'll pacify him.

He's a few strides down the hallway in his long-johns when he hears his ma call out. Her voice is like the bray of a trapped animal, muffled by the door. 'Thomas, come in here and help me!' He goes into her room and finds her lying face down on the bed in just her cotton frock. She's drawn her curtains, so the room is tinted with a greenish darkness.

'What's the matter?'

'Can you feel my back and see if there's a lump? I think I've got a hernia.'

'You don't, Ma.'

'How d'you know? You haven't felt it yet.'

'You can't get hernias in your back.'

'If you can get one in your front, then you can get one anywhere.' She winces as she tries to move, then flops her head on to her pillow. 'Come on, son. It's killing me.'

He swears that she mistakes him for a husband half the time, requesting things of him which she believes are natural, chiding him if he should balk at what she asks. If she truly were an invalid, or elderly, he'd have no hesitation to perform the tasks of caring for her, washing her and wiping her and whatnot – they'd be duties any loving son would view as obligations. But she only just turned thirty-six in February, and it strikes him as improper to be looking at the flimsy fabric of her dress where it's all snug against her, let alone to plant his fingers on her back and feel the skin beneath it. Just because he's rubbed away her aches and pains since he was young and ignorant to flesh is no good reason to maintain it in his adult life. 'I reckon you'll be fine enough to go to cards. But I can get a doctor out to see you, if you need. I'll walk there now. They'll still be open, likely.'

'No, don't bother with all that – I only want you pressing here to see if there's a bump. I can't reach round myself.' She bends her arm to show him roughly where the tender spot is. 'Please, love, help. You know I'd do the same for you. It's awful sore.'

The desperation in her tone makes him submit. He edges closer to the bed and reaches downwards, gazing at the floor until it smears into a haze. His fingers meet the deep cleft of her spine and he begins to thumb the muscles round it thoughtlessly. Her body tightens in response. 'There's nothing there,' he says.

'You're not in the right spot.'

'I'm pushing where you said it was.'

'It's higher up than that.' She says this with a wounded breathiness he finds disturbing.

One more flurry of his fingers on the tissue of her back – that's all that he can muster. He can feel her house dress ruffling where he prods around, the skin so inelastic underneath it seems as if he's kneading porridge. 'I can't feel a thing,' he says, already backing out the room. 'I'll get the aspirin for you, Ma.'

'It never helps,' she groans at him.

'Well, I can hardly do much else for you. I'm not an expert.'

'No, you always get so bloody squeamish. Like I didn't wipe your arse till you were nine years old. But fine – bring me the aspirin. I'll just have to cope, won't I?'

'You will, Ma. Like the rest of us.'

No matter how much brandy he swigs now, he isn't going to sleep. The softness of her body is an echo in his fingertips. He gets the pills for her and leaves them on the bedside table with a glass of water. 'Ta,' she says, unmoving on the mattress. 'Seen as you're so wide awake, you might as well go into town and pay that cheque in for us. No good having money you can't spend. It's on the dresser, there – d'you see it?'

'Aye, all right.' He spies it, weighted down beneath her biscuit tin of curlers. 'Should I stop in at the doctor's for you on the way, or what?'

'I'll muddle through somehow. The savings book is in the drawer.'

He's at the dresser when the realisation takes him suddenly: Joan Wyeth might be there today. It's rare that he goes into town on afternoons she's working, and he's never blessed with any errands at the post office to do. He's got to show a better aspect of himself this time, if he should see her. Try to be less reverent and faint-hearted. Talk to her as though she's made of flesh and blood and not an angel on a stained-glass windowpane. He stuffs the cheque inside the savings book and goes.

'Don't take all day,' his ma says. 'I might need your help to get my shoes on later, if I can't bend down.'

For short trips into town, he'd usually walk, but he's aware that time is sliding by and there are preparations to be made before he heads out with the cart again. How lovely would it be to have a Humber of his own? He goes around the side and gets the pushbike he inherited from Pop – a bulky thing with a substantial frame he's sure is made from gas pipes welded into shape. Although he always tries to shield it from the rain, the chain keeps getting rusty in the damp and crunches when he turns the pedals. He applies a drop of oil to it, the stuff he uses on the cart's wheels when they stiffen up, and it's enough to stop the noise. He wishes he could learn to drive, but lessons are too dear, and cars so costly to maintain – perhaps with all this money coming in from Mr Acheson, his ma might be persuaded. If he's ever going to own a shanking rig, he'd need a driving licence, after all.

It's never pleasant, cycling into town. The burning in his thighs, the constancy of motion it requires to keep a decent speed, the vigilance for obstacles and potholes. At this time of year, the weather makes it worse. The drizzle's got no heavier but he's soaked before he's even reached the high street. He climbs off the bike and walks it over the slick cobbles of the alley in between the haberdasher's and the post office, kicks out its stand and leans it in the gloom. The shopfronts up and down the street are yellowed and inviting, speckled by the rain. It's busier in town than he expected: folk in sodden overcoats are smoking under awnings and umbrellas, reading through their papers, sharing jokes, and he can see the bleary silhouettes of others through the glass of Manfield's shoe shop.

Well, they might've painted up the sign above the door, but it's still drab and cramped inside the post office, and its chalky scent reminds him of the school assembly hall. He joins the little queue before the cashiers' windows and brings out the cheque – the edges of the paper have gone damp and tattered in his pocket, but it's just about presentable. The woman in the queue before him takes some time to count the pennies in her purse to buy the stamps she needs, and so he's called towards another window – and he sees that it's Joan Wyeth who's there to serve him. All at once, the fatty steak he's eaten sinks inside his guts and he's afraid he'll chuck it up before he meets her at the counter. She's a few years older than her brother and a thousand times as pretty.

'Hello, Tom,' she says. 'Well, fancy running into you. How've you been keeping?'

'Aye, not bad. How've you been getting on?'

'Good, thanks.' She nods at what he's holding. 'That for paying in, is it?'

He slides the cheque and savings book towards her. When she sees the figure he's depositing, she blinks at him a moment, folding in her lips, then looks at him more brightly. 'Just a mo,' she says, 'I've got to get a different slip for this amount.' He watches her see-sawing hips go walking off, the narrowness of where her blouse is tucked into her pleated skirt. Returning to her register, she flashes him another smile and fusses with her fringe. She has the neatest set of teeth, blue eyes that seem to lighten every time they turn in his direction. Harry says she finished school with six O levels, which'd make it an enormous waste of her intelligence if they should marry. 'Right, I've got it now,' she says, waving the paper slip at him.

'All right. Ta.' He cannot think of more to say.

'I heard you're going to that club of Harry's later on – that right? He reckons you're quite good on the guitar.'

'Oh, he's not even heard me yet. You can't take Harry's word for anything.'

'The cheeky sod. He's always trying to have me on.'

'I mean, I play a bit. Don't know how good I am, mind you. I wanted to go down the Fisher's later, but –' Even the brisk way she stamps his ma's blue savings book and slides it back to him is graceful. 'Now I've got to work instead.' He stumbles on the words. It's almost painful just to look at her. The lamplight of the cashiers' room is paling her brown hair – it's nearly blonde around the edges. There's a fragrance coming from her: soapy, foreign, floral. He can feel the pasty dryness of his mouth. The very thought that she might listen in the darkness of the club tonight, recoiling at the tuneless quiver of his voice in song, his fingers strangling every chord – he's sweating puddles underneath his coat.

'Oh, that's a shame. I thought I'd come along for once, but now I needn't bother.' She adjusts her fringe again. 'All done.'

'Right, thanks. I'll see you, Joan.'

'Yeah, see you.'

He's already starting for the door, but pivots on his heels and says, 'Tell Harry I can't make it later, but I said hello.' His voice sounds meeker than a little boy's and he's not certain that she's heard him right. Joan creases up her face but offers him a kindly wave, then calls out to the lady waiting in the queue, 'Next, please!'

Her bright expression lingers in his mind as he steps out into the greyness of the high street and its chill. He walks until he reaches the tobacconist's and gets himself two tins of Dark Virginia and three packs of rolling papers, paying more than he would normally surrender. At the news-stand, he picks out the local paper and leafs through until he finds the listings for the Broughton cinema, but it isn't showing anything with Henry Fonda's name on it, just LAWRENCE OF ARABIA with P. O'TOOLE – he hasn't got the time to watch a film in any case. Some day, he'll ask Joan Wyeth to go with him, if he can ever muster up the nerve. That's what you're meant to do, he's told, take girls out to the pictures. The tobacconist huffs loudly when he leaves the paper on the stand.

Across the road, the woozy orange lights of Hughes's bookshop are so tempting that he can't prevent his legs from dragging him towards the window. It's not often that he's got the money to afford a new release, and he can almost smell the fresh ink of the hardbacks on display. The door chimes when he opens it. He walks in with a bashful sort of gait. He's conscious of the raggedness of his old coat, the patches on his trousers. He should've combed some Brylcreem through the tangle of his hair.

A beardy fella in a knitted vest and rolled-up sleeves is at the counter with a pair of half-moon glasses nesting in his curls. 'Good afternoon,' the fella says, not looking up.

He answers with a nod. The new editions look so clean and undisturbed that he's afraid to touch them. For a while, he hovers by the books on the front shelf, eyeing up their covers from a yard away.

'Is there something in particular you're looking for?' the fella says.

'Not really, no.' He's on his haunches now and trying to read the spines down on the bottom row. 'Do you know the book *The Outermost*?'

The fella's beardy cheeks tense up into a sort of grimace. 'You're the second bloke's been asking after that in here today. I'd never even heard of it, and then he tells me it was published with a different title. That didn't help me much. If you can remember what the author's name is, I can order in some copies, seeing as it's so popular?'

'I'm afraid I don't know either.' It appears that Mr Acheson is not a man to break a promise, which is gladdening to hear. 'I know the bloke you mean. I think he wanted it for me. Was he American?'

The beardy fella pulls the specs out of his curls and puts them on the countertop. 'I'm not entirely sure. He wasn't from round here, though. Haven't seen him in the shop before. He talked the hind legs off me.'

'Aye, that sounds like him.'

'Well, if you change your mind about that order, we'll be open in the morning. I can do it for you.'

'Ta.' A brighter thought occurs to him as he's about to leave. 'I don't suppose you've got books here about the movies? Like about the folk who make them.'

'Yes, I'm sure we've one or two. Biographies of actors mostly.'

'What about directors?'

'I'm not sure. You know there's quite a good collection of that stuff at Broughton library. You're best looking there, I'd say, but I can show you what we've got for now.' The fella takes him down the aisles of crooked shelving to a section at the back that reeks of mildew. 'Up there on the right, look. That's your lot.'

'Appreciate it.'

'Just to let you know, we close at half past four today.'

'What time's it now?'

'Gone quarter past.'

'I'll not be very long.'

The fella heads off to his station, letting him alone to have a rummage. There's a faded label on the shelf marked FILM & THEATRE in thick pencil letters. What he finds are mostly books about the lives of famous men who don't concern him – Olivier, Richardson, Gielgud, Guinness – and there's one about Merle Oberon, another about Gracie Fields, and one called *British Dramatists* which isn't worth the bother to get down. But leaning on its own at the far end, as though mis-shelved, there's one thin volume with a dark green spine that has no title. He lifts it out. A young blonde actress with red lipstick beams at him from its blue cover. *Film Parade*, it's called. *From Hollywood to London*. Must be ten years old, at least. It's full of articles by movie stars about the films they're working on and their amazing journeys to success. Flicking through, he recognises faces – Judy Garland, Gregory Peck, Dirk Bogarde – and others peer up from the page with skin like porcelain and gleaming hairdos, but he can't quite place them. When he skims the contents page, his eyes are drawn to something:

WHO WILL PLAY THE VILLAIN? ...... *Magnus Fielder*   p. 52

He reads it in the half-light of the shop's back room, gliding through the dull account of Magnus Fielder's months in

Utah on the set of *Mud and Wire*, until he lands upon a single paragraph:

> Our wonderful producer tells me I was cast as Cooper in this picture on the strength of my last role in Edgar Acheson's *The Map of Days*. I was extremely proud of my performance in that movie, as the father of the murderer, Bill Kerr. It prepared me for the challenges of playing Cooper, whom I think is even more conflicted as a character, if not quite as sympathetic; and I still believe *The Map of Days* deserved to fare much better at the box office, even though it did affirm the talent of its young director in the eyes of Hollywood.

There's no price tag on the book. He takes it to the fella at the counter, who informs him he can have it for three bob, as it's quite old – but even that seems dear for just a paragraph of text. 'I'll give you one and six for it.'

'Are you aware this is a bookshop, not the indoor market?'

'I'm aware.'

'The price is what it is. Three shillings.'

'Then I'll leave it.'

'Up to you.'

'I might come back for it another time.'

'Please do.' The beardy fella puts the book aside. 'Good afternoon, sir.'

'Aye, good afternoon.' He's flustered by the loudness of the door's chime when he drags it back, and wonders if the people left inside are laughing at his clumsiness, his ignorance. The mizzle coats his face as he collects his bike and rides off home.

He's drenched again, returning to the yard. The darkness is descending. He tries to stash the bike beneath the canopy, but water's pooling at its edge and dripping on the saddle. His ma won't let him stow it in the house, and there's no room inside the stable now he's keeping his guitar in there – he balances a scrappy sheet of plywood on the handlebars instead to stave off the rain.

The horse is looking sullen in the paddock with its mane as wet and baggy as the tresses of a mop. He leads it back into its shack and shammies it. 'Sorry, boy, I know I said we didn't have to, but we're going out again. You won't be trawling, though, just walking.' The horse breathes, apathetic, pokes its head out of the hatch. 'I'll come back in a bit to sort you out.' At least there won't be any need for shanking when they're out at sea tonight – he's earned a hundred quid before they've even left the yard, so he'll not bring the nets with him, to spare the horse's energy. He can always bring them in the morning if there's any appetite from Mr Acheson to see his working methods.

He leans round the hatch to check his ma is not there at the kitchen window. It's as dark inside the house as out. The aspirin will have eased her pain by now and she'll be fast asleep, or else she'll have the curlers in her hair and starting to get dressed for rummy. He can steal a moment for himself.

The cheap guitar is still cocooned within the saddlecloth and propped up in the corner. He unwraps it and the strings give off a thin, discordant twang. The fretboard seems a little damp beneath his fingers, and he has to tune it quickly with the horse shifting its weight about in front of him, his ear close to the sound hole. When it's right enough, he fingerpicks a C chord, adding the bass G for extra oomph (he's seen the better players at the Fisher's Rest do this). The sweetness of the chord, its sheer simplicity and brightness, is as pure to him as any sound on earth, as beautiful as any picture he has seen or can imagine, even Joan Wyeth lying sideways on the grass in sunshine with her cotton dress unbuttoned. And that clean transition to the next chord, how abundantly it rings, how naturally it answers what has come before. He finds the strain in his right hand is getting easier to manage, and the quick bite of his little finger on the thinnest string, and then the fluid run of notes up to the F and down to C again, that jouncing melody. Who taught him how to do this? Nobody. It's come from observation, learning in the thrall of others every week, and practise. On another day, he'd sing the words aloud without a care and savour that refrain – *Who wouldn't be for all the world a jolly waggoner?* – but now he has to smother it. Instead, he hums the tune. The purr of his own voice inside his chest is like the jolt of his first ciggie in the morning. For a moment, he dissolves into the song. The turning of the world is of no consequence to him. He doesn't even feel the ground beneath his boots. And then he sees the light flash on beyond the hatch. His ma's all dressed up in the kitchen, rinsing out her water glass. He stops, and bundles the guitar up in its cloth again, returns it to its hiding place. The stench of horse's piss arises from the straw-bed, fresh and pungent.

In he goes, to get himself prepared for sea a second time. The rigmarole of it is still to come: the harnessing, the cart, the flask, the oilskins and the hitching up. His ma says, 'Did you get it all paid in?' She's wearing her best frock now, the bright blue one with the yellow flowers embroidered on the collar, and she's got the curlers twisted in her hair, a ciggie fuming in her lips.

He tells her there weren't any problems with the cheque and doesn't share the detail of who served him at the cashier's window, for the simple reason that his ma believes Joan Wyeth is two-faced and superior. But if he had a stone for every lass she held in low regard, he could repave the whole of England with the pile and still have some left over to do half of Wales. 'You've made a quick recovery,' he says, and it escapes him with a tone of mockery he doesn't mean.

She walls her eyes at him. 'The aspirin took the edge off it.'

'I told you it'd do the trick.'

She folds her arms so tight it's sure to put deep wrinkles in her frock. 'You've always got to be a smart-arse, don't you, Thomas? Couldn't you just say, *It's nice to see you're feeling better.* No. You've got to tease me just for trying to manage.'

'All right, Ma. I'm sorry. Didn't mean it.'

'You'll be sorry when I'm dead and gone, I know that much. You'll miss me. And you'll even miss my aches and pains.'

'I'll miss your cooking most of all.'

She feigns her indignation, throwing the dishcloth at his face with perfect aim. It slops along his nose and hits the floor tiles. 'Shut your trap,' she says, but with a grin.

'Stop being so morbid, then. You're only thirty-six.' He wrings it out and hangs it on the tap.

'That's younger than I feel, believe me, son.' She starts unravelling a curler from her hair. 'Who's been stealing all my ciggies, by the way? I thought I had another packet in the cupboard.'

'Don't ask me,' he says, 'I'd never smoke that rubbish.' Then he brings the damp Pall Malls out of his pocket. 'I found these in the yard, though. Must've been the horse.'

She's not amused this time. 'There's something up with you. You're being – I dunno. You're acting strange.' She takes the packet, stands it on the counter, and resumes the loosening of her curlers. 'Once I get these out my hair, I'm leaving, so you'd better get a shift on. Blokes like Edgar don't like waiting round for anyone.' She takes a few steps closer, pats him gently on the cheek and pecks him on the temple. 'Done me proud today,' she says. 'You're not a bad lad, really. I did something right.' A dry lump gathers in his throat. Before he can reply, she breezes past him to the hallway with her fingers buried in her hairdo, smelling of cold cream and Odorono.

The clock is telling him it's five to five.

He changes in the lamplight of his bedroom, knowing he'll be needing a much thicker jumper and a second pair of socks.

The bath has left his skin so dry it's flaking at his elbows, but at least he doesn't have to retch at his own foulness when he peels his shirt off any more. He wears an extra thermal vest, although the tightness bothers him around the neck. Before he's finished filling up his flask and gathering what's needed for the trip, he's sweaty-browed and shining.

It's a small relief to step outside into the cold again, the fluffy drizzle. He allows the horse to feed and take on water, not so much as to discourage it from grafting, but enough so it's obliged to do its duty when it's asked. It isn't fussed about the collar or the harness going on, although it seems reluctant in its movements when he leads it to the cart and gets it hitched. He lugs the boomer out and folds the nets into a heavy bundle, leaves it all upon the stable floor beside his empty whiskets. As he lifts the rolled tarpaulin up, he finds the rusty metal box he salvaged from the beach. A flare might well be useful if it proves too dark for Mr Acheson to take his photographs. He stashes it beneath the seat and checks the fillet knife is in the bucket while he's down there. All that's left to do is fetch another set of oilskins.

From the back room, he calls out to tell his ma he's leaving. She shouts back: 'Lock that door! I'll go the front way! Don't wait up for me!' He feels around his pockets till he meets the hard shape of his house keys. 'All right, see you in the morning!' he shouts back. He has to push aside a load of musty coats from where they're hanging on the hooks, which seem to be remainders of his younger days, too small to be of benefit to anyone; they should've been donated to the Salvo's, but his ma gets sentimental when it comes to their possessions – she believes the fibres of a person's soul remain in them forever, and he's never had the meanness it would take to rid her of this daft conviction.

Pop's old oilskins are so heavy in his hands. The rope belt is still threaded in the loops of the enormous waistband, and he reckons they should fit the frame of Mr Acheson quite well. He shuts the door and throws them in the cart. But by the time he's got the horse out through the yard, the rain's no longer falling, and it seems as if the evening might just be a mild one, after all. He gets the sense that something's turning in his fortunes. All those dreary shifts at sea, gone unrewarded. All his ma's relentless praying before bedtime. Well, at last a table scrap of luck's been thrown to them to gnaw the meat off. It's been ages since he rode along this track without a grumbling dread inside his stomach, looking forward to the night.

Second Low Water

A monument is what he should've called it, not a statue, but he couldn't bring the word to mind when he was telling Mr Acheson to meet him there. It rears up in the distance now, as he comes riding through the intermittent gleam of lamp posts on the promenade: a pillar of black marble on a gravel bed, surrounded by a nest of withered wreaths and flowers. Five hundred and eleven names are listed on the stone, in memory of the local men who gave their lives in service of their country, but his father's doesn't rest amongst them. Now and then, he'll make a point of stopping at this monument to read through the inscriptions, cleaving to the hope that he might land on Patrick Weir and feel a current of affection for the man, some flash of pride. He knows his father wasn't born in Longferry, but it's comforting to have a picture to revere in his imagination.

It appears he left the yard a mite too early. Mr Acheson's not there yet, waiting for him on the gravel bed as he expected, and there isn't any movement in the lamplight. It's a strangely windless evening and the air feels damp and cumbrous. There's a low-lying hump of clouds whose edges are still visible against the purpling darkness, crawling eastwards, snuffing out the moon. His ears are deadened by the clacking of the horse's shoes upon the road, but when he stops the cart inside the lay-by, all the smothered sounds prevail. The whistle of his nose as he inhales. The creak of boards relenting to his weight. The sluice of water in the drains below. And then, a sudden clap of footsteps on the flagstones up ahead.

He sees a shadow, bounding forwards. It's too broad and

stumpy to belong to Mr Acheson, but it's approaching with a sense of purpose. An arm comes up, as though to flag him down. It's just a pudgy fella in an overcoat whose smooth bald head is glinting like a billiard ball beneath the street lamps. By the time he's made it to the cart, he's panting slightly. 'Evening, sir,' he says, his face all ruddy. 'Are you Mr Flett?' Beneath the coat, his uniform is showing: a white shirt with a dicky bow, mauve waistcoat and mauve trousers. It's the outfit from the Metropole.

'Who's asking?' he replies.

'I'm no one, just a porter from the hotel up the road. I think you know a guest of ours, a Mr Runyan?'

It takes a moment to untie his thoughts. Of course, a man like Edgar Acheson would not go checking into hotels with his real name – he'd want to be discreet. 'I know him, aye. He sent you, did he?'

'Yes, sir. He just wanted you to know he's been held up,' the porter says. 'A crown he paid me to come out and tell you – not too shabby for an evening's work.'

'I'll say.'

The porter stands there, looking at the horse with dewy eyes. 'Nice animal. Does he mind being petted?'

'It's a working horse,' he answers. 'Doesn't get much pampering.'

'Ah, well, that's a pity. Lovely-looking creature.'

He's getting irked now by this sappy porter ogling the horse with wetted lips. It's strange to hear a fella speak about an animal as though it's someone's daughter dancing at the village fete. 'That's all he told you, was it? Didn't get him very much, that crown.'

'I'm sorry – I forgot to say.' The porter looks up with a measure of embarrassment. 'He asked if you could wait for him. Just half an hour at most, he said. Feel free to have a drink and charge it to his room. The downstairs bar is very nice.'

'He's wanting me to stop at the hotel?'

'Yes, sir. That's about the gist of it.'

He sighs. 'Well, blimey, I dunno . . .' They've only got a few good hours before the tide begins to rise again, and if they're going to get out far enough to meet the shallows, they should try to leave the landing ramp by half past six. 'He'd best not take all night.' The horse snorts as he gathers up its reins.

'I don't suppose you'd let me ride back up with you?' the porter says. 'I'm knackered and I've still got ages of my shift to finish.'

'All right – perch behind me there, look, on the top-board.' It's not much of a journey, but he lets the porter climb into the cart.

'I'm grateful to you, Mr Flett.'

'It's nothing.'

They go riding off along the promenade. The dark beach spreads into an empty murk beyond the sea wall, and he feels the strangest pull in its direction. He can't help but wonder what the shrimp are doing tonight, if they'll be copious as weeds, just begging to be scraped up from the sand, or shy and meagre as they've been all season. That's why Pop would say the biggest catches are the ones you can't be there to make. The mind will taunt itself by dwelling on the could've beens – no good will ever come from those regrets.

'So, you and Mr Runyan must be friendly, then, if you don't mind me asking?' comes the porter's voice above the din of hooves. 'How come you know a Yank like him?'

'I promised you a lift, not conversation,' he replies.

'All right. Fair enough.' They ride along the road without another word, until: 'I couldn't beg a ciggie off you, could I?'

'No chance.'

'Aw, come on, I'm gasping.'

'There's a crown inside your pocket – that'll see you right.'

'I know, but our machine's bust in the lobby.'

'Pal, you're getting on my nerves.' He reaches for his tin of rollies and presents it to the fella.

'Ta. That's awful good of you.' The porter tucks one in his mouth and sparks his lighter.

Behind the modest cover of the pines, the entrance to the Metropole is newly paved and brightened by small floodlights. It's the best hotel in town, which isn't quite the honour folk believe it is, but some still speak of it in pious tones, as though to get a table there for Sunday lunch is like a benediction. As he turns into the drive, he gets a view into the upper rooms where guests have yet to close their curtains: an old lady in a furry hat is taking off her earrings at the dressing table, a glum-faced boy is writing letters on the steamy windowpane. The only place to leave the horse is in the car park, where the tarmac has a trim of grass and flowerbeds he's certain will be trampled by the time of his return. He looks for Mr Acheson's nice motor, but he doesn't spot it in the row.

'Appreciate the lift,' the porter says, and flicks his ciggie to the grass verge, jumping out. 'I'd better run back in or else the manager'll dock my wages.' The fella hurries off towards the hotel's awning, up the steps.

There's nowhere he can tie the horse's reins. 'Right then, I suppose I'll have to trust you not to scarper. Can you do that for me, eh?' He strokes its flank. 'This won't take long.' The horse just swings its tail and snorts. 'Good lad.'

Inside, the hotel's lobby is so quiet he can hear the scratch of the attendant's pen upon her notepad at the desk. She darts her eyes round where he's standing: it's as if she's trying to perforate his edges like a stamp. 'You can't be leaving horses in the car park – it's for guests,' she says, 'not animals.'

'Well, it's a guest I'm here for. Mr Runyan,' he explains, and her expression loosens.

'Oh.'

'He said that I should wait and have a drink.'

She's gathering the phone into her hand now. 'Really? Well, you'd have to wear a jacket in the Sellars Bar.'

'You're saying this won't do?' He tugs the collar of his oilskin coat.

'I meant a blazer. We've got one here that you could borrow, but it mightn't fit you very well.'

'I'll just wait over there, then. That all right by you?' He gestures to the padded ledge by the front doors, where there's a vase filled up with daffodils on a little table and a cut-glass ashtray piled with matchbooks.

She nods and puts the phone back. 'If you like, I'll have somebody bring a drink for you.'

'That's very kind. I'll have a brandy. Charged to Mr Runyan's room.'

A brightness draws across her face. She goes off down the corridor and leaves him in the silence of the lobby. From his ledge, he's got a decent angle to keep checking on the horse. The fussy methods people have of decorating places never fail to mystify him: all the dark wood furniture and chandeliers, the patterned carpet and the flowers. It gives him the same doomy feeling as the funeral parlour where they held Pop's casket for a time. Before too long, the lady strides back in to sit behind her desk. 'Your brandy's coming,' she says.

He doesn't know how long he waits there, but the brandy never comes. It's Mr Acheson who finds him first, descending the wide staircase in a rush, his fingers squeaking on the balustrade. He's loaded down with gear: a silver box that hangs from a thin strap and swings against his hip, a canvas bag, a funny wooden case. His skin seems paler, porridgy about the eyes; his hair's scruffed up and sweaty at the sides, as though he's just removed a hat. 'Thomas, buddy – Tom!' he calls. 'I'm sorry you've been waiting round for me. I got caught up.' He traipses through the lobby, almost shambles, out of puff. 'So sorry. I got held up on a call. A million plates you've got to keep on spinning in this game, or else the whole thing just collapses on you. I'll never understand why all these people think I need to listen to their dumb opinions. Either you are *with* me or you aren't. Don't screw around. Sometimes, I just want to scream and tell them where to shove their money. But it doesn't matter now. I'm glad to see the porter did his job. That guy, I tell you. Do you know how much he made me tip him? *Jesus*. What a crook!' At last, he takes an inward breath. He struggles to extract his wristwatch from his cuff, then shakes his head. 'Forgot to wind this up again. My wife would always do it every morning, and I never can remember. I should get an automatic. But anyway – I brought you something.' Tucked beneath his armpit, there's an old, slim hardback poking out. 'I couldn't find it in the store, so that's my personal copy – just ignore the scribbles in the margins. Take good care of it. I want it back, Tom, when you're done with it. No hurry, though.'

'You didn't have to do that.' He's reluctant to accept a gift that means so much, but he's respectful of the gesture, too, and doesn't want to undermine it. 'Thank you, Mr Acheson.' He takes the book and glides a thumb across the cover tenderly.

'I think it's time to call me Edgar.'

'Edgar, then. I'm grateful.' The paper jacket on the book has been removed, and both the boards are plain and faded. But the title's printed in cracked silver on the spine:

FURTHER THAN DREAMING   MILDRED ÁCS

He doesn't get a moment to consider it. The clap of Edgar's palm upon his shoulder almost knocks him backwards. 'Can we still get out there now or have I blown it? You're the one who knows the tides.'

'We've still got time,' he says, 'but not as much as I'd have liked. It's best to have some leeway. Saves a lot of fretting.'

'Then I guess we're leaving.' Edgar taps the fattened pocket of his coat, lifts out a blue glass bottle, puts it back. He pats the other side and finds what he's been looking for: a tube no bigger than his thumb. Once he gets the cap off, he inserts the tube's end in his nostril, sniffs, and sniffs again, and then repeats this in the other nostril. 'Want some?'

'No. What is it?'

'Just a little something to clear out the pipes. It keeps me focused.'

'Nah, my pipes are fine.'

'You sure?'

'I reckon so. But ta.'

Edgar stashes the inhaler in his coat again. 'Hey, where'd that porter get to? He was meant to bring me up my messages. That slimy little so-and-so. D'you see where he slunk off to?'

'No. Forget him. We should go.'

'Hang on – sorry.' Edgar turns and ambles to the lady at the front desk. 'This'll only take a minute, Tom, and then the beach is ours.'

He didn't know there was another edge to Edgar's temperament: a blunter side that's not so organised or easy-going. There's no doubt that he prefers the other version who arrives with steaks and writes him cheques, but he'll forgive a bloke his flaws if there's no malice to them. In his life so far, he's come across two reasons for a good man's failings: either he's a drinker on the quiet, like Pop was, trying to numb the bruises on his heart to get him through the week, or else he's trying to cope without a remedy at all. And even if these reasons don't apply to Edgar Acheson, some fellas are deserving of the extra rope you give them. It appears the lady at the front desk isn't flustered either. She's nodding, smiling patiently, as though she's used to managing a lot of irritated guests.

He steps outside, beneath the awning, to make sure the horse has not abandoned him as well. It's still there, gawping through the branches of the pines and likely wishing it could throw its collar off and run away. He waits upon the steps and finds a decent light to read by, opening the book. The first few pages are completely blank except for some of Edgar's clumsy pencil notes, which have been scrawled so quickly he can't understand their meaning. The next page is devoted to a poem by Rupert Brooke. *Beyond the shifting cold twilight*, he reads, *Further than laughter goes, or tears, further than dreaming, / / There'll be no port, no dawn-lit islands! But the drear / Waste darkening, and, at length, flame ultimate on the deep.* It puts him in mind of Pop's casket again, that sense of hopelessness which overwhelmed him and his ma, those mornings which had risen without invitation, day by day by day, and how he couldn't conjure any feelings for the longest time – not even sorrow, or self-pity, least of all a glimmer of contentment. But it passed.

A shape looms in the space behind him now. 'Your mother had the right idea to quit this place,' says Edgar. 'It's a very bad hotel. Right up there with the worst I've stayed in. That includes the Y in San Francisco, where I had the crap kicked out of me three times. You ready?'

'I've been ready since this afternoon.' He leads the way back to the horse, whose loyalty has surprised him, standing barely a few inches from the place he left it. For want of carrots, he rewards it with a handful of his ma's sultanas, pilfered from the baking tin before he left. It's got a sweet tooth, so it's pleased and biddable.

'Should I dump these in the back or what?' says Edgar, lifting his head out from underneath his bag straps.

'No point lugging them yourself,' he answers. 'It's two miles to the shallows.'

'I should get myself in better shape.' With slow consideration, Edgar puts the silver box down in the cart; the rest, he throws in carelessly. He stands there for a moment, turning up the collar of his woollen coat. There's now a vacancy about his gaze, as though his thoughts are lagging twenty seconds in the distance. 'Where do you want your deputy?'

'Just climb straight in and perch somewhere. There's no big secret to it. Hold on to the sides, though. It gets bumpy.' He watches Edgar stand up on the tyre and step into the cart, swinging one long leg over the top-board, dropping down. 'You know, if we were on a ship, you'd be first mate. In fact, you'd be a deckhand.'

'Well, this thing is more a wagon than a boat – that makes you sheriff where I come from.'

'If you say so.'

His new deputy sits up and leans against the board, clutching at his midriff, wincing slightly; he fetches the blue bottle from his pocket, twists the screw cap off and takes a swig. 'So what's the horse's name? I like to know who's working for me.'

'Doesn't have one. *Boy* will do.'

'That's easy to remember. Hope he doesn't mind the extra weight.'

'You'll be no bother. It's well used to grafting.' He clucks his tongue and shifts the reins until they're arcing round the car park, coming down the driveway, through the gates. They clack along the promenade towards the dark plain of the beach. The lamp lights of the pierhead seem to twitch against the sky like compass needles. After they've been going for a while, he turns to check on his companion. He finds that Edgar's on his haunches, opening the latches of the silver case between his feet. Inside, a small device is packed in foam – it's like a stubby telescope with dials and switches. 'Funny-looking camera. What's it for?' he says.

'It's just a viewfinder, that's all. It helps me get a sense of how to frame a shot. I figure I'll come back and get some proper photographs tomorrow, maybe take some meter readings for the light. It's way too dark for anything but *this* right now.' Edgar puts it to one eye and shuts the other. 'Maybe a few drawings, too, if the rain holds off. I'm trying not to overthink it. I just want to get a feeling for the place and understand it better. It's the only way to work. Let other people sweat on the logistics and stay focused on what's most important.'

They roll up to the landing ramp. 'Hold on tight back there!' he calls as they attack the slope. It's not much more than trotting pace, but it'll shock a man who's not prepared for it. The wind is so much gentler than it was this morning; still, the tyres spit sand up at their faces as they go. Without command, the horse tramps on towards the shallows, knowing what's required.

The clatter of the harness and the cart is loud enough to rouse a man from sleep. The sharpness of the salt inside the nostrils, too. That festering scent of bladderwrack, which lies along the foreshore here like clumps of hair upon a barber's floorboards. There's a strange, spasmodic crunch each time the wheels pass over razor shells and gnarls of driftwood. 'It's going to be bumpy for a bit, and then the sand gets flatter.' No response. 'Oi, Edgar – can you hear me? Get yourself a lantern, there, so you can see things better.' His companion stirs and leans down to survey the lanterns in the back. The batteries should last the night but, just in case, Pop's trusty Vaporite is packed as well. 'I'd put those oilskins on and all, if I were you. You're never far away from rain out here.'

'Yes, partner.' There's a clumsiness about the way that Edgar pulls the trousers on and ties the rope into a bow. He looks unsteady on his feet. 'You know, a few years back, I tried to tell a cowboy how to ride his horse on set – he got so pissed with me he quit. I guess my notes were kind of dumb, but I just wanted him to really *slump* into the shot. He wouldn't do it. Kept on saying how his character had grown up on a ranch and wouldn't ride that way. I had to get another stunt guy in to do it who had no experience with horses – and I wasn't happy with the shot, despite it all. I should've stuck with that first cowboy and not been so damn particular.' The jacket is the perfect size, although the hat's brim droops across his brow. He stoops to get a lantern. 'How bright is this?' When the switch is flicked, a wide beam sprays into the dark and finishes some twenty yards into the distance. 'The sea's so far away – it's perfect. I could swear it isn't even there.'

He wishes he could see the beach the way it must appear to Edgar, special and mysterious. But the parts of it which stoked his fascination as a boy – the strange withholding of the water, all the energy that you could sense but never see – have turned to ordinary components of his day. 'That's how it always is at ebb tide,' he explains. 'But even at high water, you'll do well to find the sea. It's great for kiddies building castles in the summer. Maybe twice a year, the waves'll come right up beneath the pier. That's a decent sight.' He reaches for his tin of rollies. 'Smoke?'

'No, thank you.'

'One of life's great pleasures, smoking.'

'So they tell me. But I'm happy missing out.'

'You really are.' He strikes a match and lights his ciggie, wondering about the other pleasures his companion must be used to: fancy clubs and hotel bars and poolside parties, stylish as the photographs in *Film Parade*. A lot of famous actresses, no doubt, all vying for a role in the next film. His meagre little comforts can't compete.

The horse treads on into the gloom. The judder of the cart begins to settle.

'Listen,' he calls back, 'I'd normally be out here until I catch enough to pack it in. Sometimes that takes an hour, sometimes it's more like three. But I've not brought the nets tonight, so you're in charge of where we're going.'

'Just take me on the route you'd usually take. And if I want to stop, I'll nudge you.'

'Right you are.'

'I hope you brought that chart with you.'

'Don't need it,' he says, turning. 'All in here.'

'A lot to memorise. You sure that we don't need it?'

'Put it this way, Edgar – did you need a manual for that camera you were using?' He tries to make his face look confident, assuring. 'Once it's in your head, it's in for good.'

He knocks ash off his rollie and enjoys the quiet while it lasts. If it were daytime, he could point towards the fuzzy outline of the bay a few miles south, the shrimping grounds of Broughton where they were this afternoon. The motor rigs are likely out already, working as a fleet. But there's a featherbed of mist down there, the makings of a proper fog, and there's nothing to show Edgar. Nonetheless, it gets him thinking. He could put the hundred he's been given to a better purpose – maybe get that lorry chassis and an engine, after all. How tricky could it be to drive a rig and teach himself a different method? If he brought in twice the haul each trip, he could reduce his hours at sea and spend more time at home with his guitar, improving. Then he wouldn't be too tired for courting girls like Joan or too preoccupied by earning to appreciate the company of friends. Enjoy his life instead of drifting through it. 'You might get the weather you were hoping for,' he calls into the back, where Edgar is now straddling the box-boards with his legs hinged outwards like a ladder's frame. The viewfinder is cupped in his eye socket. 'Are you pointing that at me? Give over.'

'I'm deciding if I want you in my picture, Tom.'

'You *don't*. I can't stand being photographed.'

'Well, actually, the camera likes you plenty. Not everybody has a presence like you do. I think it might just work on-screen.'

'Give over.'

'There's a role we haven't cast yet: Runyan's got a young assistant. Not a speaking part, but you'd be in a couple scenes.'

'Whatever's in that bottle you've been swigging from, it must be strong. I'm not an actor.'

'Great. Thank God! I don't like actors, and I don't need one for this. You'd only have to sit there with your horse and look the part.'

'In that case, you can pay me by the hour.'

'Ha! You got it.' Edgar's thumping laugh reverberates. 'We can negotiate your fee. I'll get your agent on the phone tomorrow. Hope he's realistic, though – the financing for this one is a little shaky. All the studios are chicken-shit and someone's got to stump up or it won't get distribution. I'm in pretty deep on this one. All my chips are on the table. It's worth it – no one's taking final cut from me this time – but, yeah, a lot's been put at stake.'

He can't pretend he understands this fully, but he gleans a semblance of its meaning: Edgar's not relying on anyone to make this film except himself, and it's expensive. 'I suppose you've got your reasons,' he replies, because that's what Harry Wyeth had said to him the day he'd traded Pop's old pocket watch for the guitar. He's never had a glimmer of regret about it, either.

'And it's for my ulcer, by the way,' Edgar says, raising the bottle, shaking it. 'Good old Milk of Magnesia.'

'Is it helping?'

'Hard to tell. It stops the burning. Too much steak and too much stress. I'm paying the price now.'

He expects what Edgar means by 'stress' is all the nervous strain that comes from trying to make a living in the movie business, or perhaps it's more the heaviness of striving to achieve his big ambitions and ideas. It's not the sort of pressure that should form a canker in his stomach, like the biting desperation of a man who can't afford to miss a shift at work or skip an hour at sea because of fever – that's what counts as normal life for most. But he supposes that an ulcer pains each man the same, no matter how he earns it. 'Ma does tend to overdo the lard,' he says. 'Too rich for some.'

'I didn't need the second one. It's not your mom's fault I got greedy.'

The wheels roll on towards the milgrims, carving up the resting water; it becomes a spray that ranges from the backboard of the cart like someone's garden sprinkler, wetting Edgar's oilskins and the lens of his viewfinder. Up ahead, the mist has thickened and it seems it's hastening towards them just as readily as they are gaining on it. The false light of the lantern tints its edges. He can feel a hand upon his shoulder. 'Can we stop a moment?' Edgar asks.

He draws rein and the horse comes to a halt. Its hot head radiates pale steam. The stillness is abrupt and overwhelming.

'Hold this for me, huh?' says Edgar, passing him the lantern. He keeps it steady and aloft while his companion opens out the wooden box upon his lap to make a painter's easel, laying a sheet of sturdy card there, brown as parcel paper. In fluid gestures, Edgar sketches what he sees in charcoal, capturing the withers of the horse, its muscled neck, the sharp tufts of its ears against the darkness; then he deepens it with grey chalk smears and flourishes of white to render the approaching fog. The drawing's finished in the time it takes his rollie to burn down. He watches his companion slide the picture in the box and start another one. 'Hold still. I'm using you for scale.' More hurried strokes with charcoal on the card. 'You know, I'm going to give the movie back its title, the original. I always liked it better, and I know the author does. It suits the story better anyway. Keep still – a few more seconds – almost done here, Tom.'

He's never wasted any thoughts on his appearance. Just what sort of figure he presents out here in his rank sea-clothes hasn't bothered him before. Now, being drawn, he's too aware of his own body and its failings. How his spine must curve while he sits at the reins, the way his grandpa's used to do. His ingrown nails begin to throb, his shoulders ache.

'It's sort of funny,' Edgar carries on, 'I feel I've got the strongest sense of what this beach could give the picture. There's a mood out here – it's absolutely right. I mean, it's like I've been out here before. It's so strange, when you read a book and you can picture all the places in it so completely, even though they're built from someone else's life and you're just like a tourist in the writer's scenery, you know –' A motion of grey chalk and then he reaches for the white again. 'Next thing, you've signed up for this huge responsibility. You've got to build that scenery again yourself from scratch. You're putting someone else's dreams inside a bottle. So you take it shot by shot. You storyboard it. It's the only way to do it. And you're trying to be faithful to two different things. I mean, you've got the writer's vision – how she wanted you to see it – and you've got the way you actually saw it in your head, the memories you brought along to fill the gaps. They're all your own. You'd be amazed how far apart those versions are sometimes. But when the book is good because the writer's taken care over her words, and when you're in no hurry with the script or to begin photography – and most of all, if you go scouting for the right locations and you don't just take the first damn beach they want to use because it's close to where the actor's bought a house, that kind of crap – that's when you find a place like this. And let me tell you, Tom, you've got to hold on to these moments when they come. These minor victories. They're what you think about when people ask you why you care so much, and why you've got to be so difficult, and why you've got to be so damn particular. I'm not *particular*: I'm loyal to the image in my head, that's all it is. I'm finished here – feel free to move now.'

The sketch is turned around for him, and though it's been dashed off mid-conversation and the shore is just a loose smudge fading into nothing at the bottom of the card, it's caught the shape of him all right, that weary slump he loathes to notice in the bathroom mirror of a morning and the dopey angle of his brow. He looks like Pop when Pop was brandied up and walking to the stable in his sleep.

'I want to go as far as we can get into that fog, Tom. Can we do that?'

'Yeah, but if it thickens up too much, the horse is going to fret.'

'Then how about we find the sea so I can get a proper look at it? We needn't hang around too long. Just head up to the edge and back.'

'That shouldn't be a bother. We've about a mile to go.'

'When should I start getting worried about all this sinking sand?'

'You shouldn't. Let me do that for you.' There are sinkpits on his mind as well, but the most dangerous ones are further west and they'll avoid a problem if they keep to his established route; there'll be no bother when the cart has breached the water – it's the saturated pools of sand along the shore they'll have to stay alert for. Those are broad and deep enough to hold a man until the sea slides in.

He clucks his tongue to set them on their way. The further out they go, the colder it will get, and salt will sting the corners of their eyes and make them weep.

'I can't believe you do this every day, Tom. It's a gruelling life you've chosen. I admire you for it. You're a better man than me.'

'It wasn't my decision,' he replies. 'I'm not complaining, mind.'

'And if your grandpa were alive, would you still do it?'

His devotion to the job has weakened, there's no doubt,

and he's much slower to respond than his allegiance should allow. What ties him to the shanker's life is not necessity, as such – a steady wage could be acquired by other means – and nor is it a sentimental gesture to the man who raised him. No, there's something more essential to it, simpler, but he can't quite isolate the reason well enough to understand it. There's a kind of gravity that holds him here, for definite, but most days he spends yearning to be free of it. The only answer he can summon is: 'It's likely I'd be playing my guitar somewhere instead. And maybe I'd have stayed in school and got something to show for it.'

'Oh yeah, like what?'

He wants to say that he was always good in school and wasn't troubled by the comprehension tests or the arithmetic – if he'd stayed, he could've managed to achieve the sort of thing that people deem impressive: neat credentials on a sheet of paper. But all that he was able to redeem from school were muddled thoughts about the world beyond the beach his grandpa knew, and an awareness of his own capacity. 'I would've had some qualifications by now,' is how he puts it.

Edgar's sipping on his medicine again. 'That's not a guarantee of anything in life. A lot of the big studio guys are straight from Harvard Business School or Princeton, and they're quick to let you know about it in a meeting. But they never have a thought worth sharing – their whole lives are built on status. More than that: they want conformity. They're terrified of what's original, because it undermines them. So they get behind what's mediocre, keep on feeding you their trash as though it's good for you. They think because they've got a corner office with a Monet on the wall they understand what art is, that it's something they appreciate because they're near to it. But all they're qualified to tell a guy like me is how to dodge the IRS or who should be my caddy at the country club.' The sand below is getting less forgiving, causing

Edgar's voice to wobble. 'Boy, the crap I've had to suffer just to get a green light for this picture. Nobody would touch it at the start. They think I'm going to burn right through their money just because my last few films went over budget – well, fine, a *long way over*. They were war films, what did they expect? They're only interested in how much something makes in theatres – that's just short-term thinking, *dumb* – I'm only interested in how it's going to be remembered. And *The Cutting Party* was a damn fine movie. Trust me, that thing will be talked about a long time after I am in my grave, and nobody will give a good goddamn who wrote the cheques to pay for it . . .'

The more that Edgar talks and swigs his tonic in between, the less it seems that he's in charge of what he's saying. All that energy and appetite for conversation have begun to seem more like a restless blather. He's like the man who's snorted too much snuff tobacco in the pub. Whatever's in the bottle can't be for an ulcer – at the very least, it isn't calming his condition.

'You should make more time to practise that guitar. Stop keeping it a secret. You don't have to be embarrassed that you play.'

'It's not that I'm embarrassed. I'm not ready yet for folk to know.'

'Well, have you ever tried out an electric one?'

'No, never.'

'That'd be the way to tell your mother. Get yourself an amp and go for it. Turn up the volume. Play at midnight. Wake the neighbours up.' Edgar gulps so thickly it appears that he might choke. His eyelids flutter. 'Hey, I just remembered who it is she likes now, by the way – my daughter. It's not Elvis any more. He's out of favour. It's Roy Orbison. Last time I checked, at least. Her mother's sent her to a boarding school to get away from me – Manhattan. I don't get to see her much.' His words trail off at last, but there's a sense that they're still motoring in Edgar's mind and it's uncomfortable for him to watch. At times, their differences bewilder him. He isn't able to appreciate the sort of problems his companion is explaining. Studios and boarding schools and the responsibilities of movie-making – it's the sort of whingeing Pop would terminate by giving him a chore to do. *Wash out that riddle and stop moaning. Patch the corner of that whisket with a bit of wax, too, while you're at it – here, just melt this candle over it. I'll sort it out when we get back.* 'I'm not musical at all,' Edgar goes on, sounding sorrowful about it. 'I've always been about the visual – that's how my memory works as well. I mean, we used to have a good piano in our house, but –' It's as if his mouth has snagged upon the words. 'It wasn't mine. My wife would play it all the time, not me. We're getting a divorce. And, I'll be honest with you, I'm not taking it so well.' He's got the nose inhaler out again. Another heavy sniff in his right nostril and he pockets it. He rises to his feet and sweeps the lantern fore and aft. 'That fog is really coming strong now, Thomas. How much longer to the sea?'

It's hard to reckon in the darkness. 'Not that far from here.' His instincts rarely fail him. 'You'll be hearing it before you see it, though.' The horse continues its obedient trudge. They're riding through a slop now and it's sticking to the creature's knees and forearms, plastering its barrel. The fog is spreading like the muck in his bathwater.

'You should see your daughter,' he says, underneath his breath. He knows his voice won't carry over the wet flurry of the tyres, the hoofing, but maybe the suggestion will go out into the evening as a kind of prayer and Edgar will receive it. Nobody should put their own success above their children's happiness – it's selfish, if you're asking him, unnatural. As a method of surviving, it's a worthwhile trade: your family's comfort in exchange for your own absence. But to not be present when you have the means – to shirk a father's duty for the sake of making art – well, that's a subtler version of abandonment. The world needs fewer men like Patrick Weir and more like Pop. He didn't think of Edgar as someone who'd need this pointing out. 'What happened with your wife, if it's not rude of me to ask?' he calls over his shoulder.

'I don't know. A difference of opinion.' His companion sits again, drumming the top-board, ruminating for a second. 'She thinks I'm hard to live with, and I think she knew that when we met – I told her I was screwed up and she'd need to manage me. But lately she's been acting like she didn't see my selfishness before. I guess I've been a little – I'm not sure how I should put it. Overwhelmed. Depressed. Despairing. That can wear a patient person down eventually. But here I am, still trying to make it up to her, and she's back in New York, pretending that I'm not the person that I used to be.'

'You ought to see your daughter more.' He offers this advice aloud now, steeled by what he's heard – they can be frank with one another. Isn't that how strangers become friends?

Edgar doesn't seem to take offence. 'I want to. Yeah, I ought to make the time, I know. But listen, Tom – it's not so easy. When you're young, you think life is a string of choices. It's either you choose this door or the other door, or jump out of the window. You don't realise that most of what'll happen to you is because of other people's choices. There's a door already opened for you, so you walk straight through it, and you wonder how you wound up on the fire escape. That's life, I'm telling you. Don't bother getting older. Art's the only way I've ever had of making any sense of it.'

The lantern light is clouded by the fog now and they've not yet reached the sea. But he can gather from the shortening gaps between the milgrims that they're close. It's getting colder, too. The wind's not buffeting his ears as normal, only salting up the creases of his face. He wants to listen for the breaking waves and rest assured that he's avoided all the sinkpits on the outward leg. It's never simple to traverse these channels in bad weather. Edgar hasn't finished talking at him, though: 'I know you lost your grandpa,' he is saying, 'so I figure you appreciate what grief can do to you – you need an outlet for it, a release valve, or it eats you from the inside out. It's cancer of the heart and mind. I lost my father seven years ago. That hit me hard, and I walked through a lot of doors I shouldn't have, because I thought they'd help me disappear the pain, you know. And I dragged other people with me. But the only thing I should've done is what I'm good at – this – pouring my whole self into a film until it all dissolves away. My wife would call that hiding, and I guess she's right. What's wrong with hiding, anyway? It worked out for the Trojans. And I –' Edgar lets this thought remain unfinished. There's a noise around them now, a purr of water that cannot be smothered by the knocks and rattles of the cart and all the horse's gummy panting. It's arrested Edgar like a sudden blast of fireworks. 'Do I hear the ocean?'

'No.'

'I'm hearing water. You don't hear it, too?'

'I hear the Irish Sea. The ocean's a few hundred miles south-west.'

'Well, hey, excuse me.' Edgar huffs. 'I should've listened more in Geography, I guess.'

'We're still a bit away. Don't get excited yet.' But when he swivels round to smile at his companion, Edgar's almost shrouded by the white swell of the fog. They're losing clear sight of the pier behind the cart. The coastal road has dipped into a swirling darkness. All of Longferry – the tall spires of its churches and the chimney-tops of terraces receding to the lights of other towns – has been snuffed out.

'How often does it get like this out here?' says Edgar, scoping past him with the viewfinder against one eye.

'We'll get a fog like this about a dozen nights a month. It's worse in daytime somehow – knocks you off your bearings more.'

Edgar nods. 'That's good. A tricky thing to show on camera, fog – it always looks a little puny in a wide shot, even with machines. But this could actually stay thick for us, and we won't have to mess around with focal length. We're going to have to light it well, but that's a problem for the crew. How long's it going to take for this to scatter?'

'That depends.'

'On what? The wind?'

'On how long you can swim to see it happen. Tide'll change much quicker than the fog shifts. Don't go thinking that the water won't get up on you – it will. No safer bet. It mightn't come out further than a mile from where it is, but it'll come.' He notices the tautening of the horse's neck, a little sideways motion of its head from right to left. There isn't much to see below except the mist between its legs, but he can tell they're slowing down – they've made it to the point where, on a normal trip, they'd stop to get the boomer out and spread the nets. It's better trained than he's been led to think, this horse. Habituated to its service.

'Does the tide go out much further, or is this the limit?'

'It's already creeping in a bit.'

'So we could shoot out here for, what, an hour or two?'

'I'd say so.'

'How far does the sea come in?'

'About a mile from here. Surprises you sometimes.'

Edgar clears his throat and spits. 'It really gets into your lungs, this salty air, huh? Well, I guess we'd have to rig something – a platform for the crew, for shelter. We could bring the actors out in trucks from back that way. Two sites: one here, one further back. I told you – once I start to think about logistics, all the joy goes out of the idea. I'm sure we'll figure out a way to make it work.'

A foam is washing the cart's tyres. 'Well, here we are. I got you here, as promised.' The grey sea rises and expands into the gauzy dark beyond. Its constant energy will always be a sight worth seeing, no matter how routinely he is faced with it. The shallows sway. The small waves falter dimly in the mist and skim across the bare sand where the horse stands, resting. 'How d'you like my office?'

Edgar laughs, already kneeling to collect another lantern. 'It's exactly what I hoped for, so far. Just the right amount of bleakness. And the water doesn't even look that deep out there – I swear it wouldn't even reach my armpits. We could really use that. Would the horse walk into it, or what?' Two beams are on the water, sweeping, and it looks so treacly and wretched in the cleanness of the fog. The space between them is becoming more opaque.

'It won't be happy with me,' he admits, 'but it'd do it.'

'Well, I'd love to get a sense of Runyan's wagon riding out there. Could we try it?'

'It's deeper than it seems, you know, and cold. The horse'll tire out and catch a chill if we stay out in it too long.'

His warning doesn't gain much of a grip on Edgar, who's already got his feet over the backboard, levering himself on to the ground. 'You take one light, I'll take the other, Tom.' He's left a lantern gleaming in the back. The viewfinder is dangling from a strap around his neck. 'You needn't ride him out too far. I only need to get a look at you.'

The ranginess of Edgar's body juts out of the fog in pieces – elbows, shoulders, knees, the soft brim of his hat. He's yellow as a dandelion in Pop's old oilskins, and his pallid face retreats into the milk of his surroundings. False light splinters in the lens of the viewfinder. He steps backwards to appraise what must be lined up in the frame. 'We'll make sure Wardrobe organises some darker clothes for Runyan,' comes his sharp voice from the mist. 'What colour is the horse's hide? It's got a lustre to it now it's got a sweat on – really great. What is it, chestnut?'

'Haven't got a clue,' he answers, reining it towards the water slowly. It obliges with a weary puff that almost sounds sarcastic. 'I'd have to check the box it came in.'

'Very funny, Tom. That's helpful.'

He lets the horse tramp on until the murky water washes at its barrel and stands higher than the cart's wheels; they can go no further without panicking the animal and he won't let his cart become a bathtub neither, so he turns them back. They've not been in the sea much longer than two minutes by his judgement – he's been counting off the horse's strides. 'Oi, Edgar!' he calls out. 'We're heading back!' But, coming round one-eighty, he can't see another lantern gleaming. No shape permeates the fog. No voice answers him. There's only the wet sputter of the horse, the cart's damp creakings. 'Edgar – are you there?'

He rides in the direction he believes is right. The fog has gathered with a concentration that perturbs him, quickening his heart. The deeper they ride into it, the less he can discern – there's just the rear end of the horse before him, carving through the eddies like the prow of some lost ship. He keeps calling, 'Edgar! Edgar! Mr Acheson!' and the silence keeps reporting back. The horse is fretting too, its tail no longer flashing.

There's a way to get his bearings: think of what's unchanged. The sea is right behind him and it comes in from the west. So, if he stays on this straight path and doesn't let the horse meander, they'll be going due east and, soon enough, they'll meet the fringes of the coastal road and surety again. Except he can't abandon Edgar, who's not used to being out here even in the most serene conditions, and the water's rising on them in their separation and communication lag. 'Wait on, boy!' He brings the horse to a quick stop.

Reaching underneath his seat, he gets the bucket out and holds it loosely. With the knife, he clangs its hollow body and it makes a disappointing clatter, less reverberant than a soup can, but it's something – a noise for Edgar to latch on to. He stays there making his commotion, whistling as loud as he can manage, but the horse gets shifty at the sound after a while and, in the breaks, no answer is forthcoming. He waits, expecting he'll hear Edgar's cry not far away or recognise some muted pulse of light in front of him, but nothing comes. Then, as he's putting back the knife and bucket, his palm lands upon the metal box, and he remembers.

It's not certain that the flare gun's going to fire if he pulls back the trigger. Hurriedly, he lifts it out and hinges it to check the cartridge isn't wet or jammed – it seems all right, though what he knows about the matter could be written on the thin edge of a rolling paper. He stands up in the cart with gun in hand, and warns the horse: 'Eh, boy – don't get yourself into a twist, all right? I'm going to make a right old noise. D'you hear me? I'll count down from ten.' At five, he points the gun towards the sky and plants his boots upon the boards as firmly as he can. 'Four . . . three . . . two . . .' He steadies his left wrist inside the clamp of his right hand. 'One.'

He squeezes on the trigger and it gives.

The sound it makes is like the sudden puncture of a tyre. The gun jolts in his grip. There's a thick tuft of fumes, an ashtray odour, and a bright red streak ascending to the heavens. The surprise is too much for the horse. It lurches forwards, spooked, and he goes reeling back against the boards. The lantern smacks his knee and flickers out. It feels as if the horse is running, and he can't get upright.

In the sky above, the flare has cast a spray of red into the darkness. The fog around him is a wall of colour, pinker, weaker, but illumined. The horse is settling, he can tell from the vibrations of the cart. Eventually, it halts and gives a snicker. Who can say how far it's run, or what direction it has taken? He lies there in the standstill with his head against the boards, examining the woozy redness that surrounds him. And he hears a faint cry in the distance: 'Ughhm, ughhm.'

He heaves himself straight up. 'Edgar!' But the voice doesn't reply. 'Hold on, I'm coming for you.' All the batteries have been knocked from the lantern, and he has to find them in the cart and thumb them in again. He climbs down to the sand and takes the horse's bridle. 'I told you not to get yourself into a twist,' he says. 'Did I not say that?'

'Ughhm.' It comes again. The voice is paling in the blanket of the fog. He can't tell where it's coming from. North-east? He tries to lead the horse in that direction. There's no time to soothe it, even though it seems disturbed, resistant. 'Come on. Walk, you lazy pony. Walk.' But it won't budge.

He strokes the long plate of its nose and finds its eyes are tensed and glassy. Breaths are pouring from its nostrils, and its tongue is hanging slack and sticky. It's been rattled and there's no consoling it until the fog clears. No amount of coaxing or brute force will shift it.

'Ughhhh.' The groaning voice is just a murmur now. North-east – he'll have to trust his ears and leave the horse there with the cart, although it pains him. Pop would always keep his thoughts collected in these situations, when the rules of nature seemed to change on them without due notice, so he tries to follow that example, settling his own mind. The idea strikes him: if he gets the loop of ochred twine he stores inside the cart for net repairs, then he can tie one end on to the horse's harness. There must be at least a ten-foot length of it left over.

'I'm not ditching you,' he tells the animal, as he attaches the stiff twine below its collar buckle. 'See? I'm coming back before high water.' He retrieves his lantern from the sand and heads north-east, or what he reasons is north-east, unspooling twine along the way.

This time, he's counting his own paces. After thirty-two, there's hardly any twine left in the bundle; and by thirty-eight, it's just a tightrope in the mist with nothing more to give. But the groan is there again, much closer. 'Urghhhh.' And he can see a smear of something on the ground – a pulsing orange light beyond the candyfloss of fog. He calls out, 'Edgar!'

'Urghhhh.'

He drops the twine and keeps on walking.

Twenty paces and he finds the other lantern toppled in the sand; its beam is dying, jittery. There's no sign of Edgar. He's lost every sense of his own bearings on the beach. The only way to judge is from the texture of the sand, which seems to him more like the corrugated plains you should encounter further from the shallows – easterly, towards the pier. It's as he's picking up the broken lantern that he notices the footprints still impressed beside it. They're so large and deep they must be Edgar's. He goes after them, half-stooped. The pink mist swirls above his boots. His eyes are stinging now. He needs the wind to rise and blow the haze away, but it's as still out here as God has ever made it. Edgar's footprints have become much fainter, and the sand is flattening out. A sheen of wetness grows. What prints were there have since dissolved. He stops to listen for the groaning voice, which doesn't come. Has he turned west?

The hopefulness drops out of him. He wishes he could see some marker that would give him a better hold on his location – knots of kelp or shell scraps, clumps of moss. But he's feeling more bewildered than he was on his first outing to the Broughton lido as a boy, lost in the stream of giddy bathers rushing to the pool, tripping on his towel until he only saw a thick parade of legs and no one helped him up until his ma appeared.

It's hard to know how long it's been since he came down the landing ramp with Edgar, but the sea won't wait for him to move before it rises up again. He chooses what he thinks is the most reasonable direction – back towards the ribbed sand and away from where it's wettest. There is nothing he can do about the horse except to pray it doesn't come to harm. And Edgar – well, he hasn't given up yet. He'll keep listening and calling out all night until the fog lifts or he drowns.

He's heading back now through his own dumb boot-prints, trying to retrace the fruitless steps that brought him here. There's a taste inside his mouth so tarry, and his vision's bleary with the burn of the flare's smoke. He treads without much thought or confidence. He keeps his ears pricked for a hint of sound. And maybe it's because he's so intent on hearing Edgar or the horse behind the fog that he forgets to look, forgets his normal trepidations, and his boot sinks as he plants it, falling through the sand as though it's pudding batter.

Down he goes with it. His full weight plunging sidelong. The viscous sand spreads over him. He cannot breathe – the air is caught within – until he springs up, buoyed by his own lightness, gasping, spitting all the gluey grit away; it clings to him, seeps in through the waistband of his trousers and his jacket. Even though the surface is below his neck, the suction braces him – he cannot move – and there's a pressure on his chest. He tries to call for help. He whistles, clucks his tongue in desperation, hoping it might lure the horse. There's no puff left inside his lungs to shout. A groan is all he can force out, a feeble 'urghhhh'.

One eye's been pasted shut, the other twinges with the scratch of sand caught in its lashes, just a slit through which he can make out the upturned world. So this is it – the way that he'll be taken off to meet his maker. Not an imprint made upon another person's memory. No important words preserved. Just shrimp, great basket-loads of shrimp to show for his existence, and he didn't even get to sing one tune down at the Fisher's Rest.

He's sure that he can hear the sea approaching now. Or is it just a trick his mind is playing, like when you hold a cockleshell against your ear? All the fight's gone out of him – he doesn't even struggle – he just waits. After a while, his body hangs there, floating in the sinkpit's mouth, and he can breathe more easily. He groans again for help. Again. Again. But there's no point in crying to an empty shore. He lets his eyes close, wondering what his ma will do without him, how she'll puzzle over the guitar when she discovers where it's stashed away. He drifts towards his end. The water's shushing him. It's lapping at his ears. The sea has come at last to bury him.

Then – *tkka-tkka-tkka* – in the distance – something.

Tkka-tkka-tkka.

Bright lights penetrate the fog, too harsh to keep his eyes on.

Tkka-tkka-tkka.

It's the racket of an engine. Drawing closer. *Tkka-tkka-tkka.* And, squinting, he can see the boxy shape of it – a shed on wheels – a motor rig. It's slicing through the mist and he's been captured in its headlights. *Tkka-tkka-tkka.*

He's lifted upwards. Somebody has snagged him by the collar, pulling him towards the rig. He feels the pressure of the sand release and slurp. And then he's lying on the solid ground again, half conscious, and a stocky woman's standing over him as though she's looking at a foal that's just been birthed.

'Isch schh scghhh,' the woman says, and repeats it. There's a chequered scarf across her nose and mouth. Her hair is long and matted, and the loose fit of her overalls cannot conceal the shape of her: it seems she's got a pregnant belly. Even so, she heaves him up and makes a crutch out of her shoulder. Step by weary step, they walk towards the rig. Its motor rumbles on behind the swirling fog. The hollow of its shed is yellow and inviting. 'Isch schh scghhh,' the woman tells him, pointing to the door. It's clear she has no English, even the most basic words. 'Isch schh ich scghhhhh.'

'All right,' he answers, and he climbs on to the platform, rolls himself inside. The warmth envelops him: the passive engine heat against his back and the persistent steam of the rig's boiler. He's so grateful to her, so relieved, that he can hardly stay awake.

The woman bangs the floorboards. 'Issch cchh!'

'What?'

'Isch chh chh!'

He levers himself up. 'I don't know what you're saying.'

The door slides shut. A latch is brought down on the other side.

'Don't leave!' He thumps the wood, but there's no strength left in his arms. 'We need to find my friend. I need to get back home.'

The motor's throttle revs and then the rig begins to move. Equipment clatters – riddles hanging on the walls from hooks, great metal trays and rusty boomer poles and buckets. There's a hatch that opens to the driver's cab, but it's drawn shut. Outside the little window by the boiler, there is only fog, part-lit. He can't tell if they're heading back towards the pier or if the woman's driving south to where the other rigs park up in Broughton of an evening. Either way, he's glad to be indoors and heading somewhere. Maybe Edgar's back at his hotel by now and fretting over him, or sitting in some other fella's rig and gulping ulcer medicine.

They seem to drive forever. His clothes are soaked and scratchy where the sand is hardening. He stays warm, leaning on the boiler, thinking of his ma playing her rummy and the money all this effort has secured. Providing is surviving. He should try not to forget that from now on. The joggle of the boiler's housing where he rests his head is pacifying, but he wants to smoke. The rollies in his tin are likely sodden, and his matches, too. He doesn't bother digging for them.

The rig stops suddenly. Its engine dies. They're back on

solid ground. He hears the latch unlock. The door slides open and the woman in her bandit's mask is speaking gibberish. 'Schhhg ichhh schh.' She reaches out her hand and, when he takes it, pulls him forwards. 'Schfffschffff.' This time, she points at where she must be wanting him to go.

They're in amongst the sand dunes, where the fog is thin and pink, and a fringe of marram grass encloses them and spikes the sky. As he drops down to meet the sand, it seems so dry and loose. The woman leads him onwards. He takes slow, unsteady strides. Ahead now, he can see a campfire blazing – a pyramid of driftwood billowing red smoke. 'Where've you taken me?' he begs the woman, who says nothing, only keeps on trudging. There, beyond the fire, his horse stands at the brow of a high dune. It looks well, contented to be grazing, and it's harnessed to the cart still. 'Schhhhfff,' the woman says again, and waits so he can have a moment to attend to the animal – he's teary at the sight of it, and when he puts a hand upon its flank, he feels a surge of reassurance. 'Hello, boy,' he murmurs. 'Told you, didn't I?' The horse stands there impassively, the way a horse is meant to do. It's chewing on a thatch of foliage and small white flowers. He turns back to the woman. 'Thank you. Can you understand me?' He brings his palm up to his heart so no interpretation's needed. 'Thank you.'

She just nods at him – 'Ichh schffgh' – and carries on. The horse stays idle, happy, while she takes him on a winding path that scales the dunes.

The slope is steep and soft beneath his boots. He grabs hold of the marram grass to keep his balance, but the woman climbs it without effort, gravid as she is. Her bare feet leave thick imprints where they land. Dry sand cascades – he follows in her trail, step after step, and doesn't even feel the sharp bite of his ingrown nails, just heaviness, a melancholy that's bone-deep and sedating. The fog is weakening the higher up he gets, and he can see the woman waiting at the dune's peak on her haunches, giving him the hurry-up.

He staggers to the top, expecting he'll be faced with a descent as sheer as he's just climbed. Instead, he finds a shallow incline where the sandhills level out to form a vast, uneven plain. The lushness of it staggers him. Each sandy knoll stands thick with foliage as green as parkland, and the ghost-white heads of flowers hang down in clusters so abundant you would think that snow had fallen yesterday. A path cleaves through its middle. At the far end, there's a modest building — timber-sided on a base of bricks; it seems to be a farmhouse or a country inn. Pink smoke is venting from its chimney. All its windows glimmer warmly and the melancholy freight he's dragged uphill feels lesser at the sight of where he's heading.

The woman shows the way, meandering ahead. Further on, the path begins to taper; then they're trekking knee-deep through the flowers along a clearing thinner than a railing. With each step, the building's shape solidifies before him — it's a run-down pub, the sort that opens only for a few determined regulars. They might be further from Longferry than he thought, maybe as far as Port St Anne's. He can't make out the sign above the door. The woman starts to hum a tune, a bouncy, childish song she doesn't seem to know in full, repeating the same cheery train of notes.

Before too long, they reach the grassy yard where cars have worn smooth patches in the turf and engine parts and lorry tyres lay buried in the weeds. He can read it now, the ruined sign against the weathered paintwork of the building's face:

THE FOGBELL

The woman's humming isn't tuneless, but he's glad to have the quiet back until they go inside. The front door opens straight into a dingy snug — it's not much different from the

Fisher's Rest, all brass and darkly varnished wood and tired upholstery. No one's standing at the bar, and nobody is at the pumps to serve. It has the ordinary odours of a thousand other pubs: stale beer and ashtrays overflowing. There's the atmosphere of closing time about it, though a fire is burning strongly in the hearth as they pass through. The woman stops beside it, bends to lift an armful of dried flowers from a short basket on the floor, and drops them in the flames, which burn a little pinkly, puffing ruddy smoke.

She waves him on, beyond the bar and through a corridor towards the lavvies. There's another doorway to the left of where she stands now, waiting for him with her hands upon the shelf of her round belly. And he hears it gliding down the darkened staircase she's impelling him to climb: a rhythmic swell of music in the room above. Guitar, a fiddle and a concertina, and the smack of something more percussive. He goes upstairs, towards a wobbly blade of light. The woman doesn't follow, but she's still below him, peering from the bottom step when he looks back.

The lower panel of the door has been kicked through. It's swinging in the draught so much its latch is clattering. The music brightens, echoes as he nears it.

A folk group is rehearsing in the empty function room. Their seats are in a circle, close together, worn black cases open at their feet. The fella on guitar is slumped, his back towards the doorway, jouncing both his knees to match the energetic beat. They're practising a reel. It strikes him that the fiddler and the concertina player are so alike they could be brothers: sunken-eyed and sallow, with grey sprigs of hair receding into baldness. They're the first to notice him approaching and they seem to lose their concentration, trying to relay a message to the other fella while the reel grows lazier and more chaotic. The fiddler gives a whistle and withdraws his bow. The concertina wheezes to a halt. And then the other fella turns with his guitar still on his lap and clocks what they've been trying to make him see. 'All right, lads – we'll carry on tomorrow. None of us has got that second change worked out yet. We've got lots to do to get this polished up. See you in the morning, eh?'

The brothers nod and murmur in assent and pack away their instruments. They amble to the doorway, brushing past him with expressions of displeasure, and trudge off down the stairs.

'Don't mind that pair,' the other fella says. He's standing with the neck of his guitar in hand. 'They've never had no manners. Come on over here and have a sit with me so I can talk to you. I had a feeling you'd be coming, but you've caught me on the hop. Come on and give those ingrown nails a rest.' He drags an empty chair across the floorboards.

'How d'you know about my toenails?'

'It's the way you're standing. We both suffer from the same affliction.' He returns to his own seat. 'They're beggars, aren't they, how you think you've got them beat and then the pain keeps coming back. But they've not given me a moment's gyp since I've been living up this way. You sitting down or what? Let's have a conversation, you and me. It's overdue.'

'I need to get back home,' he answers.

'Still in that same cottage, are you, with your ma? Now there's a handsome woman, even if she's carrying a few more stone these days. She wears it very well, mind you.'

He's sure they've never met before. There's nothing of this fella he can trace within his memory, no specific fondness or aversion, but he seems to know his ma. She's had a fair few callers down the years; this fella must be one of them. 'If I recognised you, I'd have said hello,' he tells him. Still, he goes to take a seat. Under the room's lights, he gets a better view of this strange fella's leathery complexion, how the shaven scalp above his ears is ridged with scabs. He's wearing a brown suit without a shirt, so when he's upright in his chair his scrawny stomach puckers, furred and pasty.

'How far away is this – past Broughton?' He's concerned for Edgar and the horse, and wondering at the mess that's waiting for him once he gets back home.

'Further,' says the fella.

'Port St Anne's – as far as that?'

'Aye, that'll do. Why not?'

There's hardly a few yards between them now and he can feel the pressure of the fella's scrutiny, his little rabbit's eyes turned sidewards underneath his wiry brows. 'You don't recognise me, do you, lad? There's no good reason why you should – but still, it hurts my sense of pride a bit. Here, let me see if I can't make us more acquainted. Go on – have a go.' The fella's thrusting out the old guitar towards him. 'Play "The Jolly Waggoner", I'll sing along. I know the words.'

'No, ta.'

'Don't act so shy, lad. You're not fooling me.'

He accepts the instrument but doesn't let his fingers touch the fretboard. It's better than his own cheap box of wood at home, the neck so shined and hefty – but it's strung right-handed.

'Go on. I know somebody's got you thinking you're a leftie. But forget all that, just play. It's only C to G, then C to F. The old tunes are the best, if you ask me, but who'm I telling? You already know.'

The instrument is too impressive to resist, curving on his thigh as though it's made to measure. His fingers are so pliant, obedient. What gave him the idea he was left-handed? This is easier than blinking. He attempts the change to G and its reverberations put a tremor in the floor.

'Aye, that's it. You're getting in the spirit now.'

He fingerpicks the sequence of the chords once through and then, compelled by something in the tone of the guitar, he opens up his heart to sing. '*When I first went a-waggoning, a-waggoning I did go / Well, it filled my poor dear mother's heart with sorrow, grief and woe / And many are the hardships that since I've undergone . . .*' He's coming round the verse's bend into the chorus now, and it surprises him when he arrives, because the fella belts it out with him, the lower harmony: '*Sing whoa, me lads, sing whoa / Drive on, me lads, drive on / Who wouldn't be for all the world a jolly waggoner?*'

The fella gives a nod. A look of dim amusement settles on his face. 'Sounding good, lad. Keep that tempo. I can see your picking's slacking off. Stay with it now.'

He carries on, accompanied not only by the fella's harmonies, but by the stamp of his boot's sole upon the floor, the meaty slaps of palms against his knees:

> *When it's pelting down with rain, me lads, I get wetted to the skin*
> *But I bear it with contented heart until I reach the inn*
> *And I sit down a-drinking with the landlord and his kin*
> *Sing whoa, me lads, sing whoa*
> *Drive on, me lads, drive on*
> *Who wouldn't be for all the world a jolly waggoner?*

> *Well, things is greatly altered now and waggons few are seen*
> *The world's turned topsy-turvy, lads, and things is run by steam*
> *And the whole world passes 'fore me just like a morning dream*
> *Sing whoa, me lads, sing whoa*
> *Drive on, me lads, drive on*
> *Who wouldn't be for all the world a jolly waggoner?*
> *A jolly waggoner.*

At the finish of the song, he's overcome by satisfaction with his own performance, not a lyric garbled or forgotten, nor a chord misplaced. He didn't even strike a wrong note with his fingerpicking or miss out the higher melody towards the end.

'First time you've sung in front of someone?' The fella reaches over to reclaim his instrument. 'You did a proper job of it and all. A decent set of pipes you've got on you.'

'Ta, but it was sounding so much better with your harmonies on top.'

The fella's wiping down the fretboard with his jacket sleeve where sweat has moistened it. 'Our voices blend, that's why. A natural fit. It's funny how it goes. I mean, we've never even met before, have we? And yet it's like I've sung with you for years.' The fella leans back in his chair with the guitar against his ribcage. He plucks a little trill of notes – *daddle diddle dum, dah doo dah* – and says, 'D'you know this one as well or do you need to read it off the sheet?'

Daddle diddle dum.

'Never come across it, no,' he answers.

Diddle daddle dum, doo dah dah.

The fella's fingers work the frets so ably, strumming with his right hand so the chords pursue the riff and fill it out. But then he thuds his other hand against the strings abruptly, turns the instrument around until it's flat upon his lap. 'Well, there's loads of time for me to teach you it. We've all the practice time we ever need in here – I know the landlord.'

'Oh yeah?'

'Aye. That girl who brought you here – well, that's his daughter. She and I are close. Poor thing was born without a tongue, can you believe that rotten luck? But I take care of her, since he's too hard of heart to do it, and he lets us have this room to play in. I suppose it's fair reward. She's quite a bloody handful.'

There's a noticeable glint of mischief in the fella's eyes. He scratches at the skin over his ears. 'Did you ever think of being in a group with someone, lad? I've been in this one since

I was roundabout your age and I'm not sure we've got much better. Good enough to pack a folk club out, as long as it's not too far south of home. No money in it. Never could give up the day job. But it's given me more joy than otherwise life's served me up. You know exactly what I mean, though, don't you? I can see you do.'

'Suppose you're right,' he says. 'I never thought much of it – I'm still learning how to play. Not good enough to join a group.'

'Well, not yet perhaps. But give it time.' The fella spins the guitar round on his lap again and strums it absent-mindedly. 'Listen, I've been waiting years for you to pay a visit, and I'd nearly given up. It's selfish, but I wanted you to come here as a nipper – thought you might've done a few times, but your grandpa and your ma had other plans. So I've been patient. Very patient.'

'I don't remember you.' He states it bluntly, seeing if the fella takes offence or not. 'How d'you know my ma?'

'Can't say I do, not any more. We haven't spoken since she was fifteen. I tell you what, though, she was quite a girl back then. It pained me just to look at her. My God.' The fella's strumming chords now. 'Come on, sing this with me. You should know it.'

But he doesn't recognise the tune at all. He watches the chord changes, trying to follow. 'I've not heard it.'

'Course you have. It's one of our old standards, this. Everybody knows it in these parts.'

'I'm telling you, I don't.'

'All right, then. Suit yourself.' The fella mutes the strings against his flattened hand, aggrieved. 'I know you've heard it, though. I know you know me, too, but you're not ready to admit it. Did you think you were alone out there? It's my voice you've been hearing every morning when you're on that beach, lad. Who d'you think was whispering? The wind? Give it a rest. That voice was mine. Whenever you get tired and bored and all you want to do is lay in bed and read a book, that's me you're hearing. When you traded in your grandpa's precious watch for that old shoebox you've been calling a guitar – I know you heard me telling you. Don't act all coy about it now. That flare gun didn't just wash up in your nets, you know? It's military issue, that. I left it there for you to find. And who d'you think was egging you along to take the Yankee's money? You were dead excited – can't fool me. I know the parts you hide away from other people. They all come from me. I put them in your blood and you should thank me for them.'

He's ready to stand up and smack the fella in the mouth, defend himself and all the people who've been there to raise him up. He's never failed to understand the truth when it was spoken, and he understands it now. It's Patrick Weir he's talking to. He's rooted to his chair. His father's never been this close, and he can only sit there, gazing back. 'Nobody told me that you played,' he says. 'Nobody said that you were in a group.'

'They didn't have to, did they? I could tell you on my own.'

'They said you were a teacher – was it true?'

'You could say I was a jack of trades. I taught a bit of English. Geography. A bit of History, too. They milked out every penny they could get from me, and then they made me join the army. Well, I wasn't much cut out for that.'

'You're nothing like I pictured you.'

'And how'd you picture me? Shot dead? Lying in a ditch somewhere? That's not far from the truth.'

Patrick Weir is smiling at him. He cannot believe how much it's lifting him. That melancholy weight – where has it gone? Dissolved by one frank conversation. 'I suppose I always thought you'd look more – I dunno. More like the devil people said.'

'Well, have a look at me. Decide it for yourself. Am I the devil? I've no horns, look,' Patrick Weir says, showing him the topside of his scabby head. 'It doesn't matter now. You're here, and I can teach you everything you need. I've missed being a teacher. I can make a proper singer out of you, I know it – and we'll have you picking that guitar like it's a harp. You wait and see. I've got a trick or two to show you. We've got all the time we need now, you and me.'

'I should be getting home soon.'

'Nah, come on now – stay awhile. A night or two. See how you like it here. There's loads of room in this place for you. Always has been.'

'I dunno. Ma's on her own. She'll worry.'

'It'll do her good – remind her what's important.'

'I dunno.'

'Ah, come on, lad. We've just got started with rehearsals. I can run you through the charts, and you could join us for a couple of numbers. We've a gig tomorrow night, up here. Me and the boys. We'll pack this whole place out.'

He's twitching at the prospect. The idea of playing in a band with his own father – it would be a kind of miracle. His blood is fizzing up again. He can't sit still or keep the jitters out his voice. 'I'm sorry, I –' An upward force is squeezing him below the armpits. It's as if he's being raised up by a winch. A digging of the skin. A tight pain in between the shoulder blades. But there's nobody in the room besides his father, who's hurrying towards him now with something in his hand – it's just a sheet of paper. 'Please. We need you. Stay and join us, lad. Things won't be the same if you go back.' His head's awash and bleary. There's a foul taste on his tongue like varnish. Patrick Weir is holding up the page for him to see. 'Come down and hear us play, at least. They've never had a better group round here, I'm telling you. We're worth the ticket. Trust me.' It's a little photostatted poster for his band's performance. 'Please, son. It'd mean the world.'

Upstairs at the Fogbell
Friday Night
SEASCRAPER

'I want to, but –'

'Listen, tell you what, I'll add your name there, underneath. How's that? "And special guest: Tom Flett." Sounds good to me. D'you like that?'

'*Thomas* –'

'Sorry?'

'Thomas.'

'Well, all right. No skin off my nose. Should've been Tom Weir, if I'd had my way. Up to you, son.'

'Thomas.'

'Like I said, it makes no difference.'

'Thomas,' he says back again. '*I know you hear me. Thomas.*' There's a sharp sting on his cheek, repeating. Smack, smack, smack. '*Thomas, breathe, come on now. Cough it up.*' A drumbeat on his back. He's calling in a voice that's not his own.

His father rushes at him with a face of such disgust it's fearsome, and he snatches at the poster. 'What's the matter?'

He can't gather a reply. The words won't come.

'Sod off – don't you waste my time. Sod off, then, if you're going. I'm tired of begging. But I'm telling you, I won't be here when you come back. I'm done with waiting round for you.' The poster's scrunched inside his fist. 'I've got no use for you now, anyway. The others never wanted you to join. We're better on our own. You make your own luck in this life and you're not getting mine.' The room's bare light bulb flickers overhead. His father drops the poster at his feet and stamps on it. He's hacking up some phlegm, or trying to. His throat's too dry. Too tight. The light bulb fizzles. 'Help me, then,' his father says. 'You do it for me – spit – I've nothing left. Spit on my grave, why don't you?'

For a moment, he can't summon any moisture to his mouth. He can only lean and sputter dust.

Thomas. Spit it out now.

There's a shudder in his belly. Something's curdled in there, wanting to escape. The feeling surges and erupts. He retches out a stream of salty water, gritty on his teeth. The light diminishes, and then it's gone.

'All right, get it up – you got it, buddy – good, that's better,' says a shaky voice beside him. He's looking up at Edgar Acheson again, whose hand is squeezing his shoulder. 'Boy, you had me worried for a second.'

The fog's as thick as ever, but the redness has dispersed. He's lying on his side in sodden, heavy clothes, a burning in his windpipe. The sea is close – its waves are breaking on the shore not far from where he rests his head now, sliding in beneath the mist.

Edgar's crouching, out of puff. 'We ought to get you off this beach before the water gets much higher. Can you walk?'

He nods, although his body seems incapable. It takes a moment, and the crook of Edgar's arm, to get him upright. He remembers setting off from home and what came after. He recalls the shock of falling, and the pressure, and the desperation and relief. 'I left . . .' he tries to say, and starts again, 'I left the horse somewhere.'

'I know.'

He feels the blood returning to his legs.

'I got him back, don't worry.' Edgar shows what's in his grip: a length of twine coiled round his palm like kite-string on a stick. 'It took me longer than it should have, but I found my way to you eventually. I didn't mean to lose you in the first place. I was just – shit, I dunno. One minute I was testing out the angle for a shot, the next I couldn't see my own damn shoes when I looked down. This fog is crazy. It was only when you set that flare off that I knew where I should go. I dropped my lantern. I was calling for you, but I guess you couldn't hear.'

'I couldn't.'

'Well, believe me – I was calling out for you.'

They take it slowly, stride by stride, until he spies the dark frame of the horse behind the fog; he's never been so glad to look upon the dopey animal. It gives an apathetic shuffle of its hooves as he approaches.

'You're shivering, you know,' says Edgar. 'Want my jacket?'

'Nah, I'll be all right.'

'You sure?'

'I'm fine now. Ta.' Except that tune is nagging him, that *daddle diddle dum*. He recalls the song more clearly than the colour of his father's eyes: the melody and shape of it, the rise and fall.

'The fog's not lifting. Can you get us back in this?'

'I've got my bearings now. The sea's behind us. We just have to keep it that way.' He strokes the horse's nose awhile. 'Let's get you home and watered.' Reaching in below the seat, he takes his knife out of the bucket, cuts the twine away, but leaves a little strip of it still hanging on the buckle to remind him.

Edgar climbs into the cart and sighs. 'I thought you said you'd keep me out of trouble.' His laughter is so bright and strange, it's reassuring. 'I should get my money back. You fell into the first damn sinkpit that you found.'

'You weren't supposed to wander off like that.' He takes his seat, draws in the reins. 'The horse got het up by the flare, and you were gone. I've never had a problem with a sinkpit in my life until this evening.'

'It was my fault. I take full responsibility.'

'Bloody right it was.'

Edgar's checking his equipment is undamaged. Satisfied, he leans against the boards and stretches out his back. 'You know, I almost slipped a disc just trying to get you out of there. It didn't seem that deep, and you were kind of floating in it – but the sea was coming in, and your head was flopping down already. It was looking pretty serious for a while, but then I found my strength. I only knew what I should do because I saw it in a movie – I crawled out on my belly just to reach you.'

'How'd you pull me out?'

'I had that rope around my pants. I guess I hooked it under you and pulled.'

'I'm sorry that I put you through it.'

'Don't thank me – thank *Lawrence of Arabia*. I didn't even like that movie, but I guess it taught me stuff I didn't realise.' Edgar's sounding winded. There's a haunted slump about his shoulders. 'How're you feeling?'

'I've been worse, I reckon.' He's a little sore around the chest and has the underlying sort of chill that might yet spike into a fever, but he's not in bad condition. It's his mind he's worried for – he hasn't quite emerged yet from the place he was before. The presence of his father lingers in his mind, as though the sun has passed behind a cloud; still there, still coming back, but when? He's thankful that he didn't drown and spared his ma the cost of burial, another trench of mourning she does not deserve. But it's a sad day when you finally get to meet your father and he's more than you expected – not the callous devil you had built him up to be – and then he's gone again before you've had a chance to tell him so. That tune of his, though: it won't leave in such a hurry. *Daddle diddle dum*.

'D'you see a flask back there?' he calls behind. 'A bit of coffee ought to see me right.'

'Sure thing. Hold on.'

He waits for Edgar to retrieve it.

'Pour me out a cup?'

The coffee gushes out into the lid and Edgar hands it to him, steaming. All the satisfying sweetness coats his gullet as he gulps it down in one. 'Well, that'll do for now. Until there's brandy.'

'We should go and drink my hotel dry.'
'Sounds tempting.'
'If you need to take a shower, you can use mine.'
'I dunno –'
'You're right. I'll book a separate room for you.'
'Don't bother. I've to get the horse back.'
'Well, I guess I'll have to drink alone tonight. I should be used to it by now, but company is always better.' Edgar wags the flask at him. 'D'you mind if I partake?'
'Nah, fill your boots.'

They ride off, eastwards – he's quite sure it's eastwards – through the wall of fog. Behind him, Edgar slurps his coffee, making noises of appreciation, while the horse takes slower paces than it usually does when bound for home. His father's song is lilting in his head. He has the urge to whistle it aloud, but he can't keep his lips from trembling long enough to form the notes, although the blast of coffee's warming him. *We'll have you picking that guitar like it's a harp.* He can't pretend it wasn't meaningful to know his father's voice in concert with his own, how good it might've been. Perhaps his appetite for music was inborn and he's been drowning it at sea each morning he comes out here.

On they go, not speaking of their destination, or of anything at all. Just like the old days with his grandpa, heeding every knock and clatter of the harness and the cart. With only Edgar's lantern glowing at half-strength, it's hard to see too far ahead of them. He'd try to spark the Vaporite except his matches are soaked through. The horse is glumly quiet, going through its motions. It won't be long until they see the pier, the old town surfacing again on the horizon.

As the tyres roll on, beginning their quick judder on the more compacted sand (they're heading in the right direction now), he listens to the music, trying to recall the shapes his father's fingers made upon the fretboard. He needs to get back home and fathom out that melody. Until then he can only harbour it and let no piece of it escape.

By and by, the horse's gait begins to stiffen. It hoofs along with more assurance, as though sensing more familiar ground beneath its shoes. The lantern's casting light no stronger than a birthday candle, but the fog is dissipating. He's pining for a smoke, a drink, another feed, a bath. The wind is getting up now slightly, billowing his sleeves. And then it happens – the first sign of surety – a spread of yellow and the hump of coastline he knows better than his own backyard. Longferry. The promenade. How long has it been beautiful? 'Over there – d'you see it?'

'Well, thank goodness,' Edgar says. 'Though I had every faith, of course.'

'Yeah, right.' A soberness has gripped him at the sight of home. 'I know a lot went wrong tonight – that's down to me. Don't blame the beach. It wouldn't have to be that way next time you come. It's still a place like nowhere else. Don't rule it out because I got you in a fix.'

'No chance of that. I like this town of yours just fine.' The pier lights wobble in the darkness, growing bigger as they ride. 'I think we'll have to do it with a modest crew and get our casting right – no prima donnas wanting twenty takes a scene. Perhaps a second unit could be trusted to do most of it. But, the way I see it, if an actor falls into a sinkpit like you did, that's something we could use. I'd never waste a happy accident like that. It's magic on the screen. I'm still committed to this place.'

'I'm glad.' The wet drag of his jumper and the thermals underneath are chilling him. He reasons he's spent half the day in saturated clothes, and it'll be a wonder if he doesn't catch pneumonia by the morning. One way or another, he'll be dead before he's twenty-one if he keeps shanking with a cart out here. He's scratching up a living every day and something has to change. A motor rig would be a decent start, but more than that. He needs to reconcile the things he wants with what he's able to achieve, and work out if this life that he's inherited from Pop is worth bestowing when he's finished. Who will he bestow it to, at any rate? There's no one in the queue behind him. He's been closer to the grave than he has ever been to marriage. He can't even tell Joan Wyeth that he likes her. It can't stay that way forever.

They're more or less where they began. The tyres crush the razor shells and whip sand at their eyes. The landing ramp has never felt more solid. Up they go, along the coastal road, on to the promenade, its easy tarmac and its downy lamplight. This far east, the fog is nothing but a twist of pale smoke in the air. They ride beyond the monument – 'You sure about that room, Tom? Nice hot shower would do you good' – and he's too adrift in his own thoughts to recognise how much his teeth are chattering beneath the *daddle diddle dum* inside his head. He can't let go of it. He's got to write it down.

The windows of the Metropole are screened by curtains now and nobody is smoking at the sills or on the entrance steps. He steers the horse into the car park, brings it to a stop. 'Last call for that shower,' says Edgar, standing tall behind him.

'Nah, I'm better off at home,' he answers. 'Get a fire going, have a drink or two, I'll be all right.'

'Then I guess this is goodnight.'

They shake on it. 'Thanks for being there to save me.'

'Likewise.' Edgar crouches to collect his bag and equipment. 'I'd love to get some photographs out there tomorrow morning, get those meter readings, too.' He climbs down from the cart and looks up with his head aslant. 'Are you amenable to that?'

'As long as I don't have a fever.'

'Have to get my money's worth before I go, right?'

'Well, low water's – let me think a second.' Every Sunday he commits the week of tides to memory so he never has to check again, but now the numbers are a tangle. There's a simple rule of thumb to it: add twenty minutes to the time of first low water yesterday. 'It's twenty-five past six, or thereabouts.'

'Meet here at six o'clock?'

'If I'm still breathing then.' He takes the reins. 'I'll see you, Edgar.'

'Good man. See you.'

Edgar backs off with his cases, heading for the front steps while the horse begins its ponderous turn out of the car park; and when he finds that Edgar is still standing there to wave him off, he knows they've passed beyond the territory of strangers, into something more like friendship. Even Harry Wyeth has never waited to say cheerio to him – the first to go, the last to show his face, and always grudging that he had to leave his pudding on the table. Edgar gives a mock salute as they roll by and pass the gateposts.

The entire journey home from town is fraught with shivering. He's been colder in his life – those dismal days alone in winter, when the milgrims were iced over, were much worse than this – but the more he tells himself he's got no reason to be shaking, the more he seems to tremble. It's the shock, that's what it is. Not from dropping through the sand or choking on seawater. Shock from looking in his father's eyes, from living in the echo of his bastard tune.

At last, he's coming down the track to his own house, a dark blot in the blankness of the night. His ma's not home to warm it for him. It looks near decrepit, charmless as a gravestone gone to weeds. He veers into the yard and whoas the horse, gets down to relieve it of the cart and disconnects the harness. It's a battle to perform what's usually routine: getting the horse bedded in the stable, fed and watered, all the gear unloaded. Once he's laboured through it, he hangs up the collar on its hook and grabs the neck of his guitar, discards the saddlecloth. He almost snaps his door key in the stiff old lock. He flicks the kitchen light on, doesn't even bother slipping off his boots or oilskins, walking sand-prints down their hallway to the front room, where he settles the guitar and kneels beside the hearth to start a fire. When the kindling's got the coals alight, he goes to strip his sodden clothes off in his bedroom, putting on as many laundered things as he can gather, wrapping the wool blanket round his shoulders till he feels cocooned. Some brandy's what he needs. He ambles to the kitchen, snatching the half-bottle of the Hennessy from the bottom cupboard by the cooker, and a tin of his tobacco from the drawer. Beside the fire in the front room, he lies flat on his back, rolling ciggies on his chest with jitter-fingers, lighting one. The smoke enlivens him and calms him in one inward breath. He swigs the brandy like it's fizzy pop, just lying there, while time smears round him, and the music plays on, *daddle diddle dum, dah doo dah*, until the shivering subsides and there's an inch of brandy left to drink. He's warm enough to stand. A word floats up from nowhere, driftwood passing by within his reach – *seascraper* – and it seems to fit the pattern of his father's tune, the scaffold of the melody. The moment he receives it in his mind, he understands where it belongs, what he should do with it.

He fetches his guitar and sits with it, cross-legged by the flames. It's slightly out of tune, but he's not fussed correcting it. He searches for the simple riff, that *daddle diddle dum*, hitting every awkward, ugly note until he's picked it out, remembering the placement of his father's hands to fashion the right chords. The brandy's gone before he's found the proper order – intro, verse and chorus, back again – and he's smoked two rollies into stubs before he's even thought of how to write it down. He gets his ma's good ballpoint pen and draws the chords as pictures, each one like a tiny game of noughts and crosses, jotting it upon a sheet of parcel paper, which was all that he could filch from his ma's room in such a hurry.

In a heavy scribble at the top, he puts SEASCRAPER, underlines it twice, as he was told to do with schoolwork. Other words descend from it the longer he sits looking at it, and he writes them down unthinkingly.

> At first light we wake
> to gulls in the shallows
> tack up our horses
> pack up the cart
>
> The pier is bright
> with lamps still burning
> once we've arrived
> we're so nearly departed
>
> Lord, give me life enough to do this again,
> to rise with the tide in the morning at Longferry
> Let me go home with the whiskets full of the shrimp
> Bury me here in these waters
> so I can be
> a seascraper
> a seascraper forever

It bleeds out of him so quickly. He's already dreamed the music. All he has to do is hang his feelings on the frame of it, make each word resonate with the guitar's melodic changes, let them gain their own momentum. He's expressing all the things he couldn't say to Pop, but he's not certain who he's telling – anyone who'll listen. No, he's talking to himself, the boy he used to be. He's writing the cart shanker's gospel so it doesn't die with him unspoken.

> After a mile and a half or more
> we bring out the boomers

> whistle tunes into the wind
> as we drag the nets
>
> It's only our horses' breath out there
> and steam from the boilers
> drifting like thoughts of men
> too tired to raise a debt
>
> Lord, it's a hard life, son, I know that it is,
> to rise with the tide in the morning at Longferry
> Let me go home with the whiskets full of the shrimp
> Bury me here in these waters so I can be
> a seascraper
> a seascraper
> a seascraper
> a seascraper forever

The pen has worn a callus on his knuckle by the time he's done. He sings it back the full way through, and then once more. It leaves him so wrung out with pride and sorrow, grief and satisfaction, that he can't accept it came from his own hand. He lies back on the floor, depleted. There's no shaking any more, no chill within his marrow, only soreness and fatigue, the anaesthetic spread of brandy seizing him. But what if he's unable to remember how the tune goes come tomorrow? Wouldn't that just be his worthless luck.

He's been awake too long. The fire sputters next to him. He ought to pull the guard across in case a coal drops out and burns the house down in his sleep. He ought to wait up for his ma. He ought to check the back door's locked. He ought to.

First Low Water

The briny smell of bacon frying rouses him. His eyes twitch open to the sight of cold grey ashes in the grate. There's an ache in his right side from hip to shoulder, and a hay-stuffed dryness to his gullet. Someone has replaced his body with a scarecrow's overnight, that's how he feels, considering the layers of clothes he's sweated through, the clammy coolness of his forehead. Then he gets a stronger whiff of bacon and he hears his ma saying, 'Goodness me, the drunkard wakes.' He brings his head up from the floorboards, rolls halfway to find her in Pop's rocker, cradled in its steady motion. She's not sat in it for years. 'There's a sarnie and cup of tea there. Something told me you'd want feeding. Had yourself a heavy night, did you? Must be a pint of brandy you've been sleeping off – I hope that was the end of it.'

He pads around to find his rollies and lights up before he answers. 'Thanks, Ma, I'll just need a minute, I'm a bit under the weather.'

'I should say so, aye.'

He cannot bear the thought of eating yet, although he's hungry. The incessant noises of the rocking chair are agitating. But the tea's a welcome prospect. He stands up and his knees click, loudly, painlessly. It's as he's reaching to collect the mug from where she's left it on the table that he sees it's resting on the parcel paper with his scribbled words and diagrams – and his guitar is flat upon the sofa in plain view of her, the varnish dulled by fingermarks, scratched up in a former life by Harry's belt. The lamplight in their front room seems to wobble for a moment. He expects some great deposit of embarrassment will fall on him, that shame will urge him to remove what's there – spill tea all over that condemning scrap of paper, throw his blanket on the instrument before she notices – but it's too late for that. And, strangely, he's not fearful or ashamed at all. He lifts the mug and necks the tepid tea, picks up the sheet of words he can remember writing in the haze of night-time. He's got no recollection of their substance, only that one phrase he underlined, *seascraper*, and if his ma knows of his secrets now, so be it. There's no reason to be sorry. He's just desperate for a moment's quiet so he can check the melody's still present in his mind, still there, each little piece of it, oh please be there. And when it surfaces again, he almost cries out with relief.

'Does Mozart want brown sauce or red this morning?' his ma asks. She cannot hide the needle in her voice.

He turns to look at her, says nothing back.

'As far as things you're keeping from me goes, I reckon this'd be the last I would've thought about. But I dunno – suppose I should be glad it's not a load of nudie pictures or some lass's dirty knickers. This seems worse. Don't ask me how. It doesn't sit well. *Here*, I mean.' She taps her breastbone. 'You've been pining to be rid of me for ages, haven't you? That's what this says to me. Like what you've got is not enough.'

He's looking down at words which say the opposite. 'You haven't read it right,' he tells her. 'Can't have done, if that's what you've got out of it.'

His ma leans backwards, rocking with her eyes alighting on him for an instant, then she springs out of the chair. She starts to gather kindling from the basket, stacks the scrappy chunks inside the empty hearth. 'Well, perhaps,' she says, attending to the ashes from last night and rising with the tray in hand. 'I'm not as clever as you, am I? I don't understand the hidden meanings like you do, we all know that. But I can read, no problem with my eyes, and that says *bury me*. That's what it says. *Bury me*. Well, don't you think I might've wanted that myself? For me, not you. I could've given up all right, if I'd not had your mouth to feed and care for. Must've crossed my mind a million times. But never once through all my struggles did I turn to boozing like your grandpa did. I know you know it. Never me, and, Christ, I would've had good reason. Who'd have blamed me? Not a soul. But no, I just got told to shut my gob and carry on.' She's teary now, pink-lidded, making for the door. 'I've got to put these ashes in the bin. Sort out that fire for us – I'm getting frostbite on my toes.'

'Ma,' he says.

She stops. Sighs loudly. Turns. 'What d'you want, son? What?'

'It doesn't mean that, what you're thinking. Honest.'

'Tell me, then. What *does* it mean?'

'It's just a song. I don't know what it bloody means.'

His ma's face tightens. 'You must think I'm daft.' She's off again, into the hallway.

'Ma,' he calls, 'is this because of *him*?'

No answer.

'It's not my bloody fault, you know, if I'm so like him!'

Now she's striding back again. There's thunder in her steps, in her expression on the threshold. 'What the fuck's it got to do with *him*?' She's hardly one to swear, his ma; the foulness of it stuns him. Her tone is more dismayed than raging, but it's sharp. 'You'd best explain that, Thomas Flett, because it's hurtful. You've got no idea how much it hurts.'

And so he tells her of his night with Edgar on the beach, the fog, the swirling dark, the sinkpit, and the dream which came to him when he was stranded and passed out and almost gone. He describes to her the dingy pub amid the field of flowers, his father's skill and confidence on the guitar, the fellas in his group, the pregnant woman in the motor rig, her bandit's mask, the full confusing picture show. 'I couldn't get the tune he'd played out of my head – I had to let it out somehow, and this was how it ended up. But I'm not sure who wrote it, him or me. I swear to God, the song was there already written, tune and everything, I only had to set the wireless right to hear it. Maybe it's a knock-off of some other song, who knows? But it was Patrick Weir I stole it from, and he was talking to me like it was a tune he'd played for years.'

His ma clears her throat indignantly. She's drawing back the curtains to announce the day's begun – she likes this little ceremony, the swift collection of the fabric and the hooking of both sides into their tassels. 'Let me tell you something about Patrick Weir,' she starts, then notices the fire's still unlit. 'You haven't even got the coals on yet for me. What's happening to you, Thomas? Used to be a time I didn't have to beg so much.' She sets about the job herself with weary movements to remind him of his idleness. 'Sometimes I hear you talk and think he's talking to me. There's a way you sit, too, when you eat your meals. You've got this – dunno what you'd call it – like a flummoxed sort of face you pull when you stub out your ciggies. Drives me mad because it's just like him. You never got to see it for yourself. You couldn't have, because your grandpa wouldn't let me speak about him. I was glad enough to have this roof above my head still, and to keep you with me. I was terrified he'd make me give you up. I knew what I'd done wrong. The shame I'd caused him. After that, after something bad like that, you never really get a say in your own life. It's chosen for you, and you have to nod along and say you're grateful. No such thing as making up for it – oh no. Do as you're told from that point on, don't rock the boat. And Patrick, well, he never got to know about you – it made sense for all concerned, except, when I look back on it, except for you.' She's got the pyre of coals alight now and she warms her fingers at the grate; and, wincing as she rises to her feet, she says, 'He wasn't such an awful fella – not as bad as people made him out to be. Your grandpa put him in the hospital, you know. Broken ribs and bruises, so he told me, but I reckon it was more than that. The school got wind of it, and that was Patrick done for. Never got to say goodbye to him. He went down south again and then – well, I suppose he joined up of his own accord. Shipped off to France and died. So that was that. But d'you know something? I honestly admired that man, how much he knew of things – of books and history and stuff that's talked of on the news – and it was sinful what we did, all right, plain wrong of him, I see that, but I've always thought I got the best of it and he got nothing. I kept hold of you and he lost both of us. But anyway – I'm telling you all this because I knew him and you didn't get the chance. I can't pretend I loved him, I was still too young for that, but I did like the way he made me feel, despite what folk might think. And he was quick up here and funny – never found him in a mood or angry – and I learned a lot from him in classes, more than from the others. There's some stuff I still remember of Napoleon that Patrick taught us all. It's useless to me now, of course. A waste of time to think about it, and I never think of him much neither. But I'll tell you this for certain – he was never fussed with music, son. I never even heard him whistle, let alone pick up an instrument and sing. That's all your doing.'

'You're sure about that, Ma?' By far, this is the most she's ever uttered on the subject and it's only left him mindful of how little he's been trusted to decide in his own life.

'God's honest truth, love. And I'm glad for you, I am, I mean it. You've the knack with words like he did, that's one thing you've got in common. Never had a passion for that much myself. It's nice you've got a hobby, but it won't put bread and butter in our bellies, will it, and that's what you're needed for.'

'I know it.'

She glances down at the guitar the way his horse looks back at him before they leave the yard, contemptuous and yet resigned. 'Let's hear it, then. This song.'

'Nah, not until I've practised it a bit.'

'I don't mind if you make a few mistakes. Just play it.'

'Nah, not yet. But soon.'

She shrugs. 'At least eat up your sarnie, then. You ought to have the doctor listen to your chest and all, make sure you don't pick up a wheeze. It could've been a lot worse, by the sounds of it. And there's me sat indoors all night without a clue.'

'I'm all right, Ma, I've got to –' He remembers what he promised Edgar. 'I'm supposed to take the horse out now. I said I'd be at the hotel to pick him up.'

'What time?'

'Six.'

'You'll need to get a shift on, then.'

'The sun's not up yet. Can't be much past five.'

'I reckon you've got water in your ears still. Clock in there said ten to six last time I looked. What's happened to your grandpa's watch?'

'I can't get into that. I'm late.' He doesn't even wash or brush the morning grizzle from his teeth, just scrambles to his room and gets some proper sea-clothes on: a pullover that's ragged at the shoulder seams but dry enough at least, some corduroys with eggy stains upon the knees that he drags from the heap behind the door. He finds his oilskins hanging from the bedposts, slings them on. The jacket seems as stiff as wicker; there's a bulk inside the pocket, nudging at his hipbone. He recalls what's in there, hoping that it won't be ruined, but it's sodden to the touch. The pages of the book are stuck together and the boards are soggy, studded with small lumps of sand. He reasons Edgar will be understanding, but he doesn't like the idea of returning it in such a state. There isn't time to fret about it now.

He races through his normal preparations, watering the horse and feeding it the forage, treading in a hummock of its muck to get it tacked, and brushing it so hurriedly it grumbles at the comb and shirks the collar till he settles it again. They're out too fast into the yard; there must be something that he's overlooked. The harness will need tightening up, no doubt, before they leave the landing ramp. He's failed to bring his usual provisions with him, too. But off they go, the horse and him, old pals, along the track to Longferry – beyond the neighbours he imagines sneering at the clop of hooves so early, past the waking homes of strangers and their shops, the milk van making its deliveries – rolling on towards the promenade again, where street lamps soften out the darkness, not a soul around for miles and miles it seems to him, the brown shrimp tumbling in the wash of water far away, awaiting his return, if not today then some day after, when the money's all been spent in the account on bills and debts and stuff to eat and smoke and Lord knows what his ma does with it, but he knows this much: the town feels smaller than it did when he rode through it last, the outer world seems fuller and less difficult to reach. He's added something to it now – it mightn't be much cop or good enough to get the admiration of the crowd down at the Fisher's Rest, but he can say he made it on his own, and there'll be more to come.

This little snippet of the coastline he relies on for his livelihood does not belong to him or anybody, but it's always there, preceding him, outlasting him for sure, and he can recognise his loyalty to the ghosts who walk along it – he can even manage to respect himself for being steadfast to the work – but there's no meaning in it any more. It doesn't matter to the sea who visits it, or to the shrimp who scrapes them from the sand. A song, though – well, a song belongs to someone. To whoever dreamed it up. Yesterday it wasn't even born, and now it's in the world. He can't go on ignoring what he's best at, and it isn't shanking in his grandpa's cart.

He turns in to the Metropole and leads the horse to last night's spot. It doesn't seem to mind the fact he made it trot along the tarmac when it's used to setting its own pace, and he's got nothing he can offer it except a few old currants in his trouser pocket from last night, all matted in the lint. He leaves it more or less contented.

There's a carriage clock behind the front desk in the lobby, and he sees he's nearly twenty minutes late. The hotel staff are elsewhere, but he rings the little bell and waits. Soon enough, the baldy porter steps in from the shade of the back office, looking quite dishevelled, carpet bags for eyelids, tie askew. 'You're here for Mr Runyan, I presume? Is he expecting more of you – more visitors, I mean?'

'He was. I'm running late.'

'I'll phone through to his room for you. Hang on.'

It takes a moment to connect, the porter sniffing and examining the ceiling. Then, 'Hello, yes, it's reception. There's a Mr –' Now the porter's drumming his own forehead, trying to remember. 'Sorry, there's a Mr Flett downstairs.' A pause. A nod. 'Of course. I'll do just that.' The porter puts the phone down and regards him. 'It's room eleven, third floor. You can go straight up. And if you've got another ciggie I could beg off you, I'll be your friend for life.'

He gets his tin of rollies out and lets the fella take one. 'Just as well you caught me in a decent mood.'

'Appreciate it, sir. This ought to see me right till I can nick off home.'

'Let me ask a favour in return?'

'You name it.'

'Keep a close eye on my horse out there. Make sure it doesn't trample any of your guests.'

'Will do.'

He takes the stairs, and by the second flight he needs a rest. His ingrown nails are barbing him again, the wretched things – it's probably time to get them seen to. On the landing, there's a set of watercolour paintings of the coast in faded frames but it's all scenery from somewhere foreign: ships and promontories and grown men in their swimming trunks. Along the hall, he counts off every door number until he reaches room eleven, knocks three times and stands there on the carpet, knowing he's dragged muck in on his boots someone'll have to clean after he's gone.

The door swings back, but it's not Edgar on the threshold. It's a tall and well-heeled woman in some kind of oriental blouse. She must be in her eighties. Skinny to the point where he can see the tendons in her neck and hollows where there should be flesh. She's got two cheekbones like the undersides of saucers, straight hair parted in the middle, white as chalk, cut sharply at her jawline. He can tell that she's a London sort before she even speaks: there's something insincere about the way she widens her green eyes at him, as though she's welcoming a servant. 'Mr Flett, hello, come in, come in,' she says, all prim, and backs into the room. 'I'm packing up the last of Edgar's things. I'm sorry he won't get the chance to say goodbye. He tells me you don't have a phone at home, and I suggested he could send a telegram, but here you are to save us all the effort.' She's calling to him now because he's still out in the corridor, reluctant and a fair bit vexed. 'Come in, Mr Flett, I'd rather not do this in public. Shut the door.'

He does as he's instructed, getting up the nerve to question her. 'Where's Edgar? He was wanting me to take him out for photographs. I'm late, I know it, but it's only just low water and there's time enough, if we can get a move on.'

'Yes,' she says, 'that won't be happening, I'm afraid. My son makes lots of plans, you see, and it's become my job to step in and *un*make them.' She gestures to the window, where a stern-faced fella in a business suit is sitting in the armchair. 'That's Stephen, by the way – he works for me.'

'Oh aye. Doing what?'

She seems to take delight in being pressed. 'Well, he's my travelling companion, you might say. Wherever duty takes me, it takes Stephen, too. Is that a fair depiction of you, Stephen?'

The fella nods, but not good-naturedly, and stands. 'I'll wait outside the door, boss. How long d'you think until you're ready?'

'Five, ten minutes. I'm an old hand at this conversation.'

Stephen nods again. 'Perhaps I'll go and see about his car, then.'

'Yes, good. You can have the local garage come and tow it, if you need to.'

'Right you are.' The fella glowers at him as he goes by. The door clacks open and then shuts again.

The woman is now ferreting around between the white glare of the bathroom and the bed. She's throwing Edgar's shaving kit into an open suitcase, into which she's bundled all his clothes. 'Dear old Stephen is retired police. He gets a bit bad-tempered when I make him drive too far from London. But he's very funny once you get to know him, not that Edgar would agree.'

'I take it you're his mother, then,' he says. 'I wasn't sure if he still had one.'

'Yes, I was alive last time I checked. Did I not introduce myself? How rude of me.' She drops the pair of shoes she's packing in the case and offers him her hand. 'I'm Mildred Ács.'

'You're Mildred Ács,' he parrots back at her. 'Now I know how you pronounce it – *Atch*.' He isn't fussed how oddly this must come across. Her hand's so soft and slight he hardly feels it when they shake. 'He never mentioned you exactly. But he lent me this –' He dips into his pocket for the book, presents it to her in its shameful state. 'I didn't get a chance to read much of it.'

'And what about the parts you did?' she says. 'Did you approve?'

He lowers his eyes. 'I only got to Rupert Brooke. I liked that plenty.'

She accepts the book between her thumb and middle finger, raises it as though it's someone's clump of body hair she's lifted from the plughole. 'Goodness, this is Edgar's copy. I suppose he must be fond of you. He's so protective of his notes.'

'I should've taken better care of it, I'm sorry. It was accidental.'

'I should hope it was.' She thrusts it back at him. 'You keep it.'

'No, I couldn't.'

'Trust me, if he sees it in this state, it's going to set him off again, and I don't want him agitated.'

'How d'you mean?'

'He has a tendency. You didn't notice?'

He just stands there dumbly, turning back his carousel of thoughts to where it started yesterday, each moment he spent in the thrall of Edgar's company, inspired, confounded now and then, concerned for him in all that fog alone, but marvelling for the most part at the energy with which he always spoke about his film, his work. 'He talks a lot, that's all. And fast. But I don't think that's agitation. More like passion, in my view.'

'That's nice of you, and rather generous.' She's sliding drawers out of the chest to search them for possessions, turning back the valance of the bed. 'These ratty things are still in circulation, eh?' She gets up with an aged stiffness, one more pair of shoes in hand: the scuffed black brogues that Edgar had on at the house.

'I'm not exactly sure what you're –' He stops himself, revising what he means to ask her. 'Listen, what's all this about? Where's Edgar now?'

'He's waiting in my car, if Stephen did his job correctly. Locked the doors and opened up the window just a crack. I used to do that with our little dog when we still had him.' She heads back to the bathroom, hunting for more stuff to pack, and huffs when she encounters all of Edgar's messy towels upon the floor. 'Owning dogs in New York City is an awful pain. I wouldn't recommend it. In high school, Edgar used to walk it for us at the weekends, and we'd pay him an allowance for the job. Just fifty cents, a dollar if he kept it out for longer. Anyway, he did it every weekend, good as gold. But then we learned that he was leaving the poor thing tied up outside the theatre while he went inside and watched a movie. Sometimes he would watch a triple feature, and the dog would be so docile when he brought it home, uninterested in eating. Edgar used to say it was exhausted from the walk and take his dollar with a smile.' She's throwing all the wet towels in the bathtub, tossing the used bar of soap into the waste bin. She's a conscientious woman, he can tell, and doesn't seem a stranger to hard work. 'You see, the trouble with my son – and I do love him, warts and all – is that he's always taking liberties with people's feelings – yours included, so I gather – and there comes a point when one just has to say *enough* of that, you know? That's what his daughter's done, his wife as well. You can't just give a person licence to destroy your life, no matter if he's family – in fact, *especially* then. Would you agree?'

He doesn't quite commit to an opinion. 'It depends how much you owe to those who brought you up.'

'You're obviously the loyal type. That was Sadie's downfall, too. Our dog.' She's battling to get all the case's zips and buckles fastened, so he moves to help her. 'I can manage, thank you.'

He steps back. 'What's Edgar done, exactly?'

'All the same things he's been doing for years. He's chasing after what he could've been. He's desperate to be more than he's been able to achieve, and he's still running after dreams that died so long ago he can't remember why he had them.'

'I don't think I understand –'

'Of course you don't,' she says, exasperation in her tone, 'you hardly know him.'

'He seems fine enough to me. I'd say he's more than fine.' And he goes reaching for some point of fact to qualify his verdict on the matter, but the only one that he can muster is: 'He saved my life last night. He pulled me out a sinkpit up to here, the sea was coming in, I would've drowned without him.'

'Is that so?'

'God's honest truth.'

'Well, good for Edgar. That'd be a first. He put another person's needs ahead of his for once. I wish I could've been around to see it.'

'That's a bit unfair. He cares about that little girl of his, from what I've heard.'

'You mean Louisa?'

'Aye. He carries round her picture in his wallet and he talks a lot about her. Seems to me he cares more than you think.'

This brings a moment's quiet from Mildred. She inclines her head and folds her arms, as if she's waiting for him to return a sixpence she's just dropped. 'I take it you're referring to the one from *Life*?' she says at last. 'He's carried that one everywhere for years. It makes him look good. But it's not from *Life* at all. It's from a piece they ran in *Picturegoer*. Very nice publicity, I'm sure, but not *Life* magazine.' She rubs at something she's just noticed on her fingertips: a residue from Edgar's clothes or shoes. 'And, by the way, that little girl you mentioned is at college now. She's almost done a year at Vassar. They don't speak – her mother won't allow it, though I've tried my best to calm the waters. Edgar's let them down too many times. But he plays the role of father in that photograph quite well, I'll give him that.'

He can't be sure whose word to put his faith in. Much of what he knows of Edgar's life in movies has been taken from a single paragraph in *Film Parade*, that's true. But, then again, he's always thought himself a decent judge of character, not minded to approve of folk before they've earned it. 'If you're saying I shouldn't trust him, I'm not sure that I agree with you. He hasn't done me wrong so far, and I'd still like to talk to him before he goes.' He walks towards the window, hoping for a quick view of the car park, but the angle is too sheer: he can't see Edgar or the horse.

'What I'm saying, Mr Flett, is that he isn't who you think he is.'

'Which part's a lie, then? Tell me.'

'All of it, most likely.'

'What about *The Map of Days*? That's not a lie. I read that for myself in *Film Parade*. So which part's false?'

'I've never heard of *Film Parade*. He gets a mention, does he? Well, that ought to please him.' She approaches him and gestures to the armchair. 'Look, I think you should sit down a moment, Mr Flett.'

'I'm better standing.'

'You seem tired. You're getting cross with me, and none of it's my fault.'

'I'm just a bit – I dunno what I am. Confused.'

'That's Edgar for you, sadly. Some men get the train to work: he drives a bulldozer.' With this, she seems to wait for him to laugh, as though she wants the validation or a signal of his understanding. 'Did he tell you anything about his life, or did he only barrel on at you about my book and how he's going to film it?'

'Well –'

'You needn't answer. I already know.' She's got the buckles fastened on the case now, so she pushes it aside and perches on the mattress. 'The thing you need to bear in mind is, in his younger days, my son was rather brilliant. His first film was a great success, the one you mentioned. It was very well reviewed – there was a critic, I remember, who was so effusive in his praise for Edgar's contribution. They put it on the posters – *visionary*, it said – and, goodness, did that please him! Honestly, I thought it was a well-made film and very atmospheric, though a bit unsubtle for my tastes. It wasn't an enormous hit, but it was no disaster either – it earned the studio back its money and they wanted him to make another. But the world had other plans. The world does tend to, doesn't it, in my experience.' She's brushing at the counterpane the way his ma does with their sofa cushions when she's anxious. After a long sigh, she says, 'You really want to know my son? Then have a look at this – I'll show you something.' Getting up, she goes through the frustrating rigmarole of opening the case again. 'My God, who needs this many straps and fastenings on a suitcase? It's ridiculous.' She roots amid the clothes and shoes inside and pulls a blue glass bottle from the jumble: Edgar's medicine, his Milk of Magnesia.

'He showed me that already,' he says, thinking he's a step ahead of her. 'It's for his ulcer.'

'Well, he claims that, yes. Except it's really for the side effects.' She brings another bottle from the case now, small and brown, which has a chemist's label. 'There's our culprit for you: Benzedrine. The army gave these pills out when he first arrived in France – to help him stay alert, or so they told him. I suppose they must've worked, because he wasn't shot to death. Some victory. He's been guzzling these like cows eat grass since then, and they've played havoc with his stomach. He's completely hooked on them. *I need to have my bennies, Mother, or I cannot cope*, he says. But cope with what? They've made him so unhinged. I mean, delusional.'

'You're wrong.' He can't accept this image she has painted of her son: it's not the fella who was sitting at his kitchen table yesterday and listening so intently to his stories about Pop. There was nothing to that man but patience and politeness. 'Never. He's as right as rain. I've never seen him take one pill since he's been here.' But no sooner has it left his lips, he knows how daft this statement is: they've spent so many hours apart from one another, and it's Edgar's name scrawled on the chemist's label. They were right there in his case.

She smiles at him unfavourably. 'Well, let's review it, shall we? Has he talked a million miles an hour at you about the film he's making?'

'Yeah, but –'

'Have you seen him sniffing an inhaler?'

'Yeah, a few times. Just to clear his pipes.'

'That's what he always says. It's Benzedrine as well – he likes his little top-ups. Need I get it from the bin and show you?'

'No.'

'He's very good at hiding pills so we can't find them. Puts them in the teapot, wrapped in foil. Inside his slippers. Keeps them loose inside his camera bag. I've even found them in those little pots the films come in. He's quite adept at stashing them away.'

'I might've seen him do that yesterday. I wasn't sure if it was something else, but I suppose it's true – he must've had some in the car . . .' The queasiness he had on his first day at sea with Pop is starting to come back to him: the judder of the wooden cartwheels rattling his heart, the feeling that the earth below is moving when he's standing still.

'Obviously, he's told you what the film's about. You've got a copy of my book. I'm sure he's really sold you on it, too. I know that's why he's here. The beach. It's perfect for *The Outermost*. The sea is so far out.'

'You're sounding just like him. All right, that's true.'

'And you're his guide,' she carries on, regardless of the

vindication. 'Edgar always likes to have one. You're the man who takes him out for photographs and helps him get a feel for the locale. No doubt he's paid you with a cheque. Some Hollywood amount to really turn your head. I'd better warn you, Mr Flett: that cheque is going to bounce. I'm truly sorry for the trouble. Please don't take it personally.'

'You're saying there's no film?' he answers, hearing his own desperate voice, the bootless tone of it, so childish. 'But why else would he come and drag me out my house? What did he need me for?'

'Oh dear, I wish I knew,' she says, and for a second it appears that she might weep, but no tears follow, only a faint exhalation. 'I believe he's trying to prove something to me by turning that old book of mine into a film. It's long been out of print, and no one's ever shown an interest in it but for him. He wants to resurrect the title I first gave it, too. But who would ever want to see a film about a book no one has read? He's been obsessed with it for years – it's been almost a decade – and he's still convinced that someone's going to put the money up, that actors will be keen to work with him again. It's total fantasy. I mean, what rational person's going to trust him with their money any more? He's burned too many bridges. Not to mention the insurance problem. Not one actor on the planet wants their name connected with him now.' She leans towards the bedside table for the telephone and gathers the receiver. 'If you like, I'll phone his wife and you can ask her. She can tell you what it's like to be an actress on his set. Let's wake her up if she's asleep. Why do you think she's living in Manhattan and he's here? Go on and ask her. Ask about what happened on *The Cutting Party* and the things he had her doing. Ask about *A Lesser Man* and *Rock of Ages* and – my God, the worst one – *Four Day Wonder*. Ask about the other jobs they fired him from, the crews who quit because of him, the arguments, the awful scenes he made, the baseball bat he put through someone's window, oh my gosh, *the bow and arrow*. She'll not shy from telling you.' The phone is bleating out a funny tone. She puts it down, as though it marks a little victory. 'Before the war, he might've been someone, you know – enough to get a mention in your *Film Parade*. That's finished with. I've made my peace with it. I suppose I should be grateful he came back to me at all, but I'm not sure. He's wasted all the money that his father left him, pumped it into movies we all tried to stop him making – half of them are still unfinished, some have never left his head. The son I had before the war was so much easier to love. He had so much *potential* . . . but it's all gone now.' Hurriedly, she fastens up the suitcase once again and heaves it off the bed. A solemn look comes over her. 'I like to keep him occupied. That's why I let him have the film rights for my book. I know that might sound cruel. He's better when he has a project to be getting on with – at least I know where all his thoughts are focused. Now and then, he wanders off somewhere like this, the phone rings, and I answer.'

He's been listening to her every word. What reason does he have to doubt her? There's a weariness about her voice that comes across as motherly concern; she seems to him a person who knows suffering, and he finds her genuine. But he doesn't tell her this. He's sure that he was born with a compulsion to defend whoever's being criticised: his grandpa, or his ma, or even Patrick Weir. He can't just stand there while a person's being flogged. He says, 'I take folk as I find them, and I think you've got the fella wrong.'

'You've known him for one day. Add forty-seven years to that and tell me how you feel. Stand by and watch him burn through his inheritance. Wait until he comes for yours. Then you and I can talk.'

'I'll tell you now,' he says.

'I rather think you've not been listening.'

'I've been listening fine.' He considers the right way to put it to her. 'Seems to me, if someone's brilliant, as you said he was before, then it's your job to help him be so brilliant again. And money's got sod all to do with it. Some day, if I'm lucky and I have a kid or two myself, and I believe they're good at something – even if it's laying bricks or catching shrimp like me – they'll have my full support until the end. I'd never let a day go by they didn't know that I believed in them. It doesn't matter how much money it'd cost me. Any child of mine'd be worth helping, and I think the same of yours. I've only known him for a day, that's true, but I feel better for it. I'm not sure I was awake before he came along.'

She's looking downcast now. 'Well, that's a very easy thing to say when you're so young. Life has a way of undermining all your principles as you get older.' All of Edgar's clothing has been packed, the clutter's been attended to; it's made the room feel spare and dowdy, too small for their conversation. 'Let me show you one more thing before I go,' she says, and drags the suitcase to the corner where the rest of Edgar's items are already gathered: silver case and canvas bag and wooden box. A leather folio is leaning there as well, no bigger than a newspaper. At first, she can't quite get the zip undone because so many pages have been jammed inside it. 'These are all the shots that he's imagined since he's been here. Lovely really. Some of them worth putting into frames.' They're drawings done in charcoal, coloured chalks and inks. Each one is an image of Longferry beach, or somewhere like it: more dramatic in the way that Edgar's rendered it.

He's not sure how he should react to them. 'They're bloody good,' is what he tells her. 'I don't see the problem.'

'No, well, *making* them's the easy part. Try getting him to stop.' She squeezes all the drawings back into the folio and zips it up again. 'There must be fifty more like this one in his house – they're everywhere. Just folder after folder. More out in his garage. Some of them I had to put in storage. In so many ways, he's brilliant. But his work is where he hides. I think he's always been this way. It took the war for me to notice it.' Now she gets her coat from where it's hooked upon the wardrobe's handle, puts it on. 'Again, I'm truly sorry for the bother, Mr Flett. It's left you out of pocket, I expect, so let me solve that right away.' Reflexively, she brings a little leather purse out of her coat and starts to count her notes. 'How much did you agree on?'

'I don't want it.' He's so resolute about it that it changes how he's standing, spine all straightened out, his heels together. 'I'd have done it all for free – in fact, I never should've taken payment in the first place.'

'Well, you're not a charity. He hired you for a service, didn't he? How much?' She doesn't even wait for his response, collecting what she deems a fair amount of notes and pushing them his way.

For a moment, he can only peer down at the money in her grip and think about the safety it could give him for the next few months, the burden it could lift. But he refuses it again. 'No, ta. I'd like to say goodbye to him, that's all. Make sure he knows I'm grateful. And I ought to give his book back.'

She withdraws the money, gazing at him wordlessly, with either pride or condescension, he's not sure. The purse is slipped into her coat. She turns the furry collar down where it has snagged behind her neck. She doesn't take her eyes off him until she pivots round to give the room one final sweep of her attention. 'All right, then,' she says. 'Walk down with me.'

He trails behind, along the corridor, down three flights of stairs into the lobby, where the porter's standing at the desk. 'Don't worry, Mr Flett,' the call comes out to him. 'I kept a beady eye on it. Your horse is fine and well.'

'Good on you.'

'Any time, sir.'

Over by the entrance doors, her fella Stephen's leaning with a ciggie and a china cup. He doesn't seem to notice her until she's close enough to tap his arm. 'Is everything in order, Stephen?'

'Yes, boss. We're all set.'

'Are you drinking lemon tea?'

'I am. I'm rather partial to it now. It keeps you young, they say.'

'I'll stick to coffee, then.'

'Too late for you, most likely. Some of us are still quite young at heart.'

'Indeed.' She blinks at him. 'I've left his things packed up for you, if you would be so kind . . .'

'I'll see to it. I'll get him ready for you.' Stephen stubs his ciggie on the saucer, leaves his drink upon a sideboard.

'Let me have the packet, then, before you go,' and Stephen stops beside the stairs and tosses her his box of Capstans, poker-faced. 'You know I don't like smoking in the car,' she says. 'It makes the leather go all sticky. Tell him, Mr Flett.'

'I wouldn't know,' he answers. 'But I'll smoke with you.'

The morning is still half-awoken. They go out to the steps to light their ciggies underneath the awning. She eyes the weather high above the canopy. 'Even when it's dark up here, it's grey,' she says.

'I think that's why your Edgar likes it. Part of why, at least.'

'You may be right. He's like a spider – drawn to gloom.'

'D'you want to go and see it while you're here?'

'See what?'

'The beach. I'll take you out.' He motions to the horse and cart across the car park, standing good and patient in the slight enclosure of the pines.

'They're yours?'

He nods. 'No bugger else is daft enough to bring them here. Although they seem to like it fine.'

'They're not that far away.'

'Where else was I supposed to leave them?'

'No – I meant, not far from how I pictured them when I was writing. Just a bit more up to date.'

'Well, no one's ever called them *that* before.' He smiles at her. 'Do you want taking out, then?'

'I don't think so.'

'Shame. I think you'd see he's on to something. It's got everything the story needs, so Edgar reckons.'

'That's as maybe.' She exhales a curl of smoke towards the bricks of the hotel. 'But there's a point at which my tolerance for this becomes indulgence in his fantasy.'

'Can I ask you something?'

'Go ahead.'

'How come your name is Ács and his is Acheson?'

She shrugs, but with her eyebrows. 'Well, he thought he had to make it more agreeable to Hollywood. My son can be astute like that – he understands what it requires to be accepted in America. That never mattered to my husband, but he didn't really care about acceptance either. He just wanted to provide. And Edgar's very lucky that his father could afford to prop him up so long.' She turns and looks upon his face now. 'Some day, this imaginary child of yours might phone you late at night – let's say you're in your eighties at this stage, not in your peak condition – and this child is going to scream how much he wishes you were dead because you won't re-mortgage your own home to finance his next movie. That'll be a test of your belief all right. Will you drive straight up to get him, Mr Flett, or leave him where he is – a grown man in a mess of his own making?' She drops her ciggie now and treads on it. 'Come out and say goodbye to him, by all means. I'm afraid I lied about him being in the car. I wasn't sure if I could trust you.'

She strides across the car park and he follows, past a line of motors to the bonnet of a Hillman, all its brightwork buffed so shiny he can see his horse reflected, a brown wobble in the silver. Leaning on the driver's door, cross-armed, she casts her eyes towards the hotel's rooftop, flicking up her chin as though to point at something there. He turns to take it in. A window on the second floor is lit, but weakly. Stephen waits there at the ledge; at once, he backs away into the room and Edgar comes to stand within the frame, his features washed out by the glass, his attitude unreadable; and it's this blankness that's discomfiting, the sudden regulation of his temperature. He has the look of some exotic fish resigned to the containment of its tank.

'There, you see – he's doing fine,' says Mildred.

'Doesn't seem that way to me.' He's waving up towards the window now to get some gesture of affection in return. 'Oi, Edgar! Down here!' He's flapping both his arms and hopping on the spot like some daft kid who's spied his mate across the street. But Edgar hardly moves. 'What's up with him?'

'Oh, not a thing. He's off the Benzedrine, that's all. It takes him a few days to shake the lethargy. And Stephen's influence is quite sedating, too.'

He calls up: 'I've still got your book! Come down and get it! Come and say goodbye!' and this incites something in Edgar, who attempts to lift the sash but finds it locked. Stephen hurries over to prevent him from undoing it and steers him back into the room.

'You can leave the book with me,' she says. 'I'll get it all dried out and see it's given back to him in better order. Or just keep it. Up to you. I'll give you an address to post it to when you've got through it.'

Edgar's reappeared now at the window, waving.

He waves back keenly, but it feels inadequate. They've become two strangers pantomiming fondness for each other. Perhaps that's all they ever were. Then, stepping closer to the ledge with purpose, Edgar cups the tube of his left fist against his eye and makes a winding motion with his right. He's got them in the scope of his imaginary camera and it's brought the flicker of a smile back to his face. It doesn't last. He's drawn away again, then gone from view, and Stephen comes to shut the curtains.

'There's no need to worry,' Mildred says. 'We've done this many times before. He'll be looked after. I intend to keep a tighter leash on him from this point on, as much as such a thing is possible.'

'Make sure you do,' he says, 'look after him, I mean.' He starts to wander off towards his horse, then pauses, thinking what he ought to do – something is amiss. But he concedes it's not his situation to intrude on any more, not his family disarray to manage, not his duty. Even so. 'You know, I think I *will* take that address off you. If you're still offering.'

'Absolutely. Just a moment, while I – hang on.' She gets into her car and reaches stiffly for the glovebox, coming back with nothing but a fancy-looking pen. 'I thought I had a notepad, but I've only got receipts for petrol and I'll need those. Shall I?' She holds out her hand until he realises it's the book she wants. 'I'll write it here, look, on the inside cover – all the pages are too soggy.' As she scribbles the address for him, she says, 'I've had a thought. Perhaps you might drive Edgar's car back down to Borehamwood for me? Hold on to it up here for a few days, or even a few weeks. Return it at your leisure. No big rush.'

'That sounds good,' he answers, 'except I'd have to get my licence first.'

'Oh. Silly me. I just presumed . . .' She passes him the book. 'Forget it. I can find somebody else to do it, or send Stephen back up on the train. What's your nearest station?'

'Broughton.' He inspects what's on the inside cover, making sure that he can read her handwriting. She's put an 01 number under the address. *The Lindens, Well End Road, Borehamwood,* it says. *Hertfordshire*. About two hundred miles from here, he reasons. It'd take a day, round trip. 'I know a fella, actually, who'd do it as a favour. Harry Wyeth's his name. I'll ask him.'

'All right, you can have him speak to Stephen to arrange it. Use that number.'

'I'll be coming with him, if it's all the same to you. I'd like to keep in touch with Edgar.'

She studies him, pursing her lips. 'Yes, I'd rather hope so. I don't give those details out to anyone, you know. In fact, I've grown accustomed to collecting Edgar from more hostile situations: pubs out in the sticks where he's enraged the locals, bed and breakfasts he's upended in a temper – that's the sort of thing I'm used to. I've had to pay a lot of compensation in my time, so this has almost been a pleasure. You seem genuinely to like him, Mr Flett, and that's remarkable to me. My son has never kept a friend much longer than he's kept a loaf of bread. You have my admiration.' She roots inside her coat and passes him the keys to Edgar's car. 'It's parked up round the side – you know the one?'

'I know it. Thank you.'

'Not at all. Thank *you*.' She steps away and gets into the back seat of the Hillman, winding down the window. 'One small tip for you – it's best to separate the pages while they're damp and dab them with a terry cloth, or else they'll never come apart. I speak on good authority, as someone who does all her reading in the bath.'

He gets a fleeting vision of her skinny, wrinkled body jutting from the murky water of an old tin tub like his at home, and shakes it off. 'I'll do my best to sort it out,' he says, and tries to peel apart the first two pages, which seem much too limp and delicate; the printer's ink has bled, but he can still make out the words. *Further than laughter goes, or tears, further than dreaming, there'll be no port* . . . He'll have to read the bloody thing to find out what that means, to understand what Edgar saw in it.

'Phone that number. We'll be glad to see you and this friend of yours, this –'

'Harry.'

'Yes. I'll pay your train fare home, though, and expenses. I insist on that.'

'I've only ever been as far as Liverpool by train. It might be good to see a bit of England.' He's never had much reason to, in truth. No distant relatives to speak of who would welcome him, no urgent curiosity about the south, only a distaste for London he derived from Pop and reading some of Dickens. He's got half a mind to call at Harry's right away and organise a date to make the trip.

'Until then,' Mildred says. 'Safe travels.'

'Aye, ta-ra. Suppose I'll see you soon.'

'Well, not me. But Stephen will be there. He'll be like Edgar's shadow from now on.' She scrolls her window up and leans her head back. He can sense that she's still there, observing all his movements, as he walks back to his horse and takes it by the bridle, guiding it around the car park, steering it in clumsy quarter turns across the verges and the flowerbeds and tarmac, till it's pointed in the right direction. He climbs up to his seat, collects the reins. One final look towards the Hillman, then he clucks his tongue and they're away. No sign of Edgar in the lobby as he passes by the entrance. No one waiting at the awning. He's known people come and go, and weathered every absence that was forced on him till now, some great, some lesser – this one is no heavier than any other, but he isn't sure how many more he can abide.

They ride along the coastal road, still short of traffic in the early hours. It must be getting on for seven now and Longferry's about to stir with folk accepting that another day's begun, draining their last cup in their pyjamas before work, smoking in their kitchens, shimmying around their kids to foist them off to school. The sea is so withdrawn it's nothing but a promise you'd be mad to put your faith in; it's the same old promise every ebb tide and he won't be chasing it this morning. Soon, he'll need the money. But he reckons it'll take till Monday for his ma to be informed of Edgar's bouncing cheque and he intends to make the best of it.

The Wyeths live together in a three-bed terrace on Cadogan Street. He can't recall the number, but he'll know the house by sight: it's got a bright blue door that Harry painted with leftovers from a decorating job. Normally, he wouldn't bring the cart along the cobbled roads so early of a morning – the racket tends to bother those with babies sleeping, plus the fact that Harry's neighbours once mistook him for a ragman – and the horse is now complaining, shaking its big head. 'Enough,' he tells it, 'just be glad you're here instead of out there, shanking. You've a weekend's rest ahead of you. Well earned, I know it, but we're not past Friday yet. Be good.' Climbing off, he spies the little piece of twine left on the harness from last night. He'll leave it there for good, until its ochre has washed out and all its fibres fray and he's too old to care about a sappy twist of string. Another half an hour or so and he can give the beast a proper feed and let it idle in the yard. He's hungry, too – there wasn't time to eat the sarnie his ma made and he can feel a headache brewing.

There it is, the bright blue door that he remembers, the net curtains at the downstairs window stained to yellow, dandelions splaying from the cracks between the flagstones and the brickwork. It's a narrow lane, but further up he's got a space to drive the cart into. He leaves it there untroubled. No more currants for the horse, just grains of sand now in his pockets. 'Won't be longer than ten minutes,' he says, rubbing its warm shoulder. 'I don't blame you for the attitude. Stick with me.'

He walks back to Harry's door, preparing what he'll say – it's one day's work at best, though it'll take some fast explaining. By the time he's reached the door to knock, he finds it's held ajar for him. Joan Wyeth is leaning there against the frame, all dressed up in her work clothes, hair tied back into a tail. 'I thought it must be you,' she says. 'Who else'd bring a horse down here except the coppers?'

'Sorry to disturb,' he says. 'Is Harry in? I need a word.'

'He just went down to get the *Chron*.'

Flat season starts next week. He's never been inclined to waste his money betting, but he keeps abreast of what goes on so he's not mute about the subject when he goes with Harry to the pub. 'They'll have a special on the Lincoln in it,' he says, sounding like a great authority. 'He'll want to know which horse their tipster's backing.'

'Who's your money on?'

'Don't bother asking me. I see enough of horses in the week.'

'Aye, I thought as much.' She laughs in sympathy. 'I don't know what the fuss is all about myself.' Even with no make-up on, her face should be in colour adverts in the magazines or beaming from some holiday brochure. Joan Wyeth does not belong behind a counter stamping people's savings books, he knows that much. She ought to be in *Film Parade*. 'He'll only be a tick. Come in and have a cup of tea.'

'Don't want to put you out. I'll come back later on.'

'The pot's just brewing now. My mam and dad aren't even up. You wouldn't be imposing, I could use the company.'

He can't refuse her, though his palms are sweating up already. 'Well, all right, that's good of you. Ta, Joan.'

'It's just a cup of tea, love.'

'Even so.'

She leads the way inside. How ought he to receive that little word, that 'love'? Is he just another of her brother's doomy friends in need of some cajoling? Is she only being as sweet to him as she would be with any of the punters queuing at her window in the post office? He can't be sure, but it's no hardship, hearing it.

In the Wyeths' house, the proper conversations happen in the kitchen. Many times he's been invited in while Harry's having supper with his mam and dad, the room a cloud of pipe smoke, thickened by the smell of dripping, so much laughter and good-natured teasing of each other, such awareness of whose habits grate and whose endear, and always beans left on their plates and more congealing in the pan upon the stove – a surfeit of baked beans, which Harry gets discounted from a fella at a warehouse. On the evenings Joan's been there for supper, too, she's never sat down at the table with him, leaning on the worktop with her plate instead, a ciggie in the ashtray, watching from two yards away. 'I'm not that keen on sitting when I eat,' she told him once. 'Not with this bunch of hooligans, at any rate.' So it's hardly a surprise to him when he gets seated at the table and she doesn't join him there. She lifts the woollen cosy from the pot and pours him out a cupful. 'Milk's there. Sugar. Help yourself,' she says.

He adds a healthy drop and spoons a sugar in it.

'Do you mind if I go out and paint my face? I need the hallway mirror. Got to be at work for eight.'

'Forget I'm even here.' He hopes she'll do the opposite.

She scurries past his chair into the hall. Another light goes on out there and he can see her lovely shadow dancing on the lino. He's afraid of his own stink, the rottenness he's brought into her house – is that what made her leave the room? He hasn't even washed the sand from all his nooks and creases. Then she calls to him: 'Here, Thomas, how'd you come into that money? I know I shouldn't ask, but, well – how did you?'

He's relieved she wants to talk to him at all. 'Long story, but it's sort of why I need a word with Harry. There's a fella who I met – a friend of mine, I'd say – American, except he lives down south. I did some work for him.'

'Oh aye? What kind of work?'

'Not much. Just took him out so he could see the beach.'

'You're joking.' Joan cranes her neck around the frame to look at him, applying the make-up to her cheeks with small strokes of a sponge. Her forehead's plastered with a colour somewhere between wheat and plant-pot. 'And he paid a hundred quid for that?'

'Well, not exactly.' He decides to be as honest with her as he can, but there are pieces of the truth she doesn't need to hold yet. 'He's well off – at least, his family seems to be. It's complicated. He's a film director.'

'No chance!' she calls back. 'A proper one?'

He realises that he's gloating now and doesn't care too much for how it makes him sound. But for as long as Joan's attentive to his words, he'll keep on going. 'Did you ever see *The Map of Days*?'

'No. Not heard of it.'

'Me neither. But he made it. He was in *Life* magazine – or maybe it was *Picturegoer*, I can't remember what he said.'

'If he's so rich and famous, what's he doing here? Arse end of nowhere, this.'

'He's been looking for a beach to film on, and he thought – well, I don't think it's going to happen now – but he was thinking of Longferry. That's where I come in, you see. I've got an understanding of the beach like no one else.'

For a while, there's no response to this. He hears a few brisk clicks and rattles of her implements and cases, floorboards creaking. Then she breezes back into the kitchen, all made up, hair falling at her shoulders. 'What's our Harry got to do with it, though?'

'I was hoping he could help me drive a car down south. My friend's car – he can't drive it back himself.'

'Sod Harry, I can do it.'

The idea of this delights him, but he can't let on how much. 'Oh no, it's far. We'd have to come back on the train. Same day. It's best if Harry does it. You've your job to think about and all the rest of it.'

Joan considers this. 'You're probably right. But don't dismiss it out of hand. I'm owed some time off work. I'd like to meet a film director. Is he handsome, too?'

'Ma seems to think so, if that counts.' The bluntness of her question cools the blood inside his arms and legs – they feel detached. 'He's married, though,' he puts in quickly. 'Has a daughter your age. He's quite old.'

'What's his name? I'm going to look him up.'

'It's Edgar.'

'Edgar who?'

'I'll keep that to myself for now.'

She perches on the worktop, folds her arms and cants her head. By God, she's pretty. Pretty in the dullness of the day, and pretty in the artificial lights of her own kitchen. 'Thomas Flett,' she says, and there's a coaxing manner to her voice, 'you're dead mysterious, aren't you?' She collects her handbag from the chair's arm where it's hanging, gets her ciggies out and lights one. 'So . . .' She lands her eyes on him, blinks slowly through the smoke. 'How've you been getting on with that guitar?'

'Good, actually.'

'I'm glad to hear it. Might you go down to the club next week, then?'

'Yeah, I reckon so.'

'I'll bring some friends to watch you.'

'Oh, don't do that.'

'Why not?'

He shrugs. 'I dunno. I'd be nervous even with no bugger there.'

'You're only being modest. I can tell.'

The silence after this is so tormenting. He can't summon up a word to say that doesn't sound pathetic in his head;

and what emerges, in his apprehension, is the most pathetic thing of all. 'I don't suppose you've got a terry cloth that I could use?'

'I've got a tea towel. Do you need a clean one?'

'Please, if you don't mind.'

'Why should I? It's my mam who does the washing.' She retrieves it from a drawer and hands it over. 'Getting more mysterious by the second, you are.'

'Ta.' He gets the book out of his pocket, sets it on the table. 'This belongs to Edgar, as it happens. It's the story of the film he's trying to make. The trouble is –'

'You dropped it in a puddle.'

'Worse. The sea.'

She whistles. 'Blimey.'

He begins to dab the cover boards with the clean towel, and she's intrigued enough to come and stand beside him, leaning over him so close she floats like sunshine in the edges of his vision. 'I was told this was the way to do it – I dunno if it'll work.' He peels the first page from the second gently, blotting it inside the layers of the tea towel till the fabric takes the damp. The paper seems less flimsy with it.

'Careful,' Joan says, as he peels away the next one. Either he's not quite as pungent as he fears or she's unbothered by his ripeness, as distracted by the lemon scent of her shampoo as he has been. 'We read his stuff at school,' she tells him, as he's dabbing at the words of Rupert Brooke. 'I don't know that one, though. I thought he mostly wrote about the war.'

'The book's named after it and all, look.' He lifts the spine to show her and she reads it out, her voice subdued, as though it's some strange passage from Leviticus the vicar's chosen for a service.

'What's it mean?' she says.

'Well, you're the only one I thought'd have the nous to tell me. No sense asking Harry, is there?'

She's quite pleased by this, he knows it, letting all the smoke heave out one corner of her mouth, amused. 'I haven't read the book, though, have I? I don't even know the story.'

'You can lend it off me, if I ever get it dry.'

Her hand drops down on to the page to feel it, and she gives a little hum of doubt. 'Perhaps I'm wrong, but aren't you dead if you're not dreaming? I mean, maybe what he's saying is when you're dead, there's nothing afterwards. No other place to go. No port or islands, nothing. Just a load of darkness. All your laughter and your crying can't reach it, and your dreams are over. You're just out there in the deep, alone. But maybe you don't know you are.' She digs her hip into his shoulder. 'Cheery fella, Rupert Brooke. That's put me in a lovely mood for work, that has. You finished with your cup? I'd best wash up before I leave or Mam'll murder me.' She takes it from him, drops it in the basin, runs the water. 'Not so sure what's keeping Harry. He was up late fiddling with his new contraption, trying to get it running.'

'What contraption's that, then?'

'Tape recorder. Got it out of Hinkley's.'

'Can't sit still, your brother. Always trading something old for something newer.'

'Don't I know it.' She turns round with fat clumps of Sqezy bubbles on her wrists. 'Go and have a look. He's left it out in the front room. Just have to plug it in, I think.'

'All right.' He supposes he can check the horse is still behaving while he's in there; most of all, he's desperate to prolong this unexpected time with Joan. She doesn't act the same whenever Harry's there, much less forthcoming with her thoughts and her opinions, fearful of being made the subject of her brother's jokes.

The Wyeths' front room is nothing like his own at home. There's carpet, for a start. They've got a dining table at the window with nice folding leaves draped in white lace, a vase on top with daffodils, no books in sight, just stacks of records in the radiogram, and copies of the sporting papers on the hearth to use as kindling. Harry's instruments are propped against the walls – his banjo, mandolin, guitar, a red accordion missing several of its keys. He finds the new toy on the carpet by the armchair: it's a mushroom-coloured box no smaller than a beer crate with two reels of dark brown tape and chunky plastic buttons. GRUNDIG TK 18 AUTOMATIC, says the maker's plaque upon the side. He plugs it in and turns it on – it makes a noise like an approaching tram. When he pushes down the button that says START, the reels begin to spin and Harry's voice speaks out at him, warped slightly, crackled: *'Latest training intelligence. Yesterday's principal work from all quarters . . . We shall start with Curragh. Fine. Scott's Snowcrest galloped a mile and a half, Whitadder and Waterwitch accompanying her the last six furlongs. Radicy, Euphrates and Bodder's Boy covered a mile at a nice pace; Earl's Crossing and Pinnacle colt galloped five furlongs; Greta Bridge and Knight of Lothian galloped the same distance. Smith's Skager Rack and Valerian cantered a mile. San Stefano and Fatima filly went five furlongs. McCormack and Casebourne's teams were usefully employed from four furlongs to a mile . . .'* He's reciting pieces of some old form guide in the *Sporting Chronicle*.

Joan's giddy laughter rises from the door behind him. He pushes STOP and can't help grinning at the sight of her. 'Just imagine bothering to tape all that,' she says, 'I think he's got designs on being on the radio or something daft.'

'He's only testing out what it can do.'

'Yeah, right.' She smirks. 'Then why'd he have to put on that posh voice like it's the Third Programme? Play it for us one more time, go on. The laugh'll do us good.'

A better thought occurs to him instead. It doesn't frighten him to play in front of her – not as much as it once did, and not if it obliges her to stay with him. 'D'you reckon he'd be bothered if I had a go on it?'

Her manner changes. She's no longer interested in laughing at her brother's foolings on the tape. He's got her wondering again; it's clear when she looks back at him without a blink. 'I'm giving you permission.'

'Don't you have to leave for work?'

'I've got ten minutes, still.'

He's committed now and has to see it through. 'Bear with me, then. I've got to work the nerve up.' The guitar of Harry's is much bigger at the body than he's used to and its neck seems thicker when he takes a hold of it. At least it's strung the right way up. The frets are old and blackened, but it sounds in tune. 'I need to warn you, I've not sung this more than twice from start to finish. It'll come out ragged, but you'll get the gist.'

She doesn't answer, only leans against the door-frame with a face of expectation.

'Oh blimey, now you've got me sweating.' He wipes his fingers on his trouser legs. 'I've never played for anyone before and you're the . . .'

She lets it go unspoken for a moment, then she puts it to him: 'I'm the what?'

'It doesn't matter.'

'I'm the what, Tom Flett?'

'The last I'd want to disappoint,' he says.

She dips her head towards her shoes and brings it up again with agonising slowness. 'I've a feeling that you won't,' she says. 'Don't think you have it in you.'

'I suppose we'll see.' He clears his throat and reaches for the buttons on the strange recorder. 'I think I have to twist the red one here, look.' It turns clockwise with a satisfying clunk. The reels are spinning. He can hear the buzz of something in its mechanism. 'I sort of stole the tune from someone in a dream, so you can blame him if it's not much good. It's called "Seascraper" – stole that from the dream and all. I'll probably forget the second verse, and –'

'Come on, Tom. Let's hear it.'

'All right. Fine. I'm dithering, I know.'

He plays the little riff, the *daddle diddle dum*, and stills his breath. He shuts his eyes. He sings.

There isn't any need to check on what his hands are doing – the chords are made before he's thought to move his fingers to the right positions – and the words he wrote last night return to him as freely as his ma's old nursery rhymes, his date of birth, his grandpa's list of daily chores, the bulletin of tides.

He's never sung so well before, so open-heartedly, the notes resounding in his chest and lengthening. When the final chorus ends, the riff trails off into the quiet of the room. He almost buckles in the armchair, wishing he could cram the song back in his mouth. But he leans over to press stop on the recording. There's a worry in him now, as though he's put down all his yearnings in one letter and addressed it to someone he barely knows.

'I feel I should be clapping you,' Joan says, 'but it'd seem a bit polite, you know, a bit too stingy. And I mean, you honestly came up with that yourself? No messing? If you did, you need to get it heard – I mean, it's really bloody good. I dunno what to say. I can't believe you sing so well. It's marvellous. But look at you, just wandering in all casual and shy, and you've got something like that hiding in your head.' She's flustered, meddling with the necklace under the soft collar of her blouse. 'When I get back from work, I'll have another listen to it. Don't you let our Harry tape more of his nonsense over it.' The skin above her clavicle is growing pink, abraded by her fingernails. 'I'd best get off now – sorry. You can just wait on for Harry here. My mam and dad won't mind.'

'Thanks, Joan. That means an awful lot to me, you know.'

She smiles. 'Ta-ra, then. See you later on, I hope.'

'Aye, see you soon.' He wants to go and take her by the hand, but what she's said will be enough to keep him satisfied until he knocks for her again and has the industry to ask her to the pictures. From behind the window's nets, he watches her walk off along the road, in envy of the people at her work who'll get to be with her all day while he survives on morsels of her company. He ought to ride the horse home to its paddock, have himself a wash and eat a plate of what his ma's got tinned and ready in the cupboard.

It looks brighter outside than it was when he arrived, but the sky's still grey where street lamps can't reach out to temper it. He's careful to put Harry's best guitar back in the right position by the wall, finding the small dent its head has worn into the woodchip down the years. Perhaps he ought to light the fire to heat the room up for the Wyeths, or maybe they'll get warm inside the kitchen with the cooker on? He can't decide, so he just kneels and tries to fathom how to play what he's recorded.

◀ FAST WIND

Will that take him to the place he was before? He presses it and hopes. The mechanism whirs, the reels spin quickly – he's not certain how far backwards he should go. His voice is bottled in the tape. It might have vanished by tomorrow. Time could wash it out before it's heard again.

To listen to Thomas Flett's recording of 'Seascraper', please visit:
www.benjaminwood.info/seascraper

THE YOUNG ACCOMPLICE
BENJAMIN WOOD

In the summer of 1952, Joyce and Charlie Savigear are waiting on a railway platform in the quiet English countryside. The siblings have just been released from borstal to start a new life as apprentices at Leventree, an architecture practice with a difference.

The architects who've chosen them are Florence and Arthur Mayhood, a married couple motivated to give young offenders second chances. At first, they seem to offer the Savigears a steady path to happiness. But when a menacing figure from Joyce's past comes knocking, they are lured back to the world they left behind. Will the Mayhoods' goodwill be enough to steer their young apprentices away from danger, or will the darkness of their past catch up with them?

'Tense and full of menace'

Johanna Thomas-Corr, *New Statesman*

'Britain's answer to Donna Tartt'

Sunday Times

'Benjamin Wood is the real deal . . . he is startingly good'

Guardian

On a station platform, with nothing to read,
and a four-hour train journey stretching ahead of him…

That's where the story began for Penguin founder Allen Lane.
With only 'shabby reprints of shoddy novels' on offer,
he resolved to make better books for readers everywhere.

By the time his train pulled into London, the idea was formed.
He would bring the best writing, in stylish and affordable
formats, to everyone. His books would be sold in bookstores,
stationers and tobacconists, for no more than the price
of a ten-pack of cigarettes.

And on every book would be a Penguin, a bird with a certain
'dignified flippancy', and a friendly invitation to anyone who
wished to spend their time reading.

In 1935, the first ten Penguin paperbacks were published.
Just a year later, three million Penguins had made their
way onto our shelves.

Reading was changed forever.

—

A lot has changed since 1935, including Penguin, but in the
most important ways we're still the same. We still believe that
books and reading are for everyone. And we still believe that
whether you're seeking an afternoon's escape, a vigorous debate
or a soothing bedtime story, all possibilities open with a book.

Whoever you are, whatever you're looking for,
you can find it with Penguin.